Willy and the Sea Captain

Willy and the Sea Captain

Sandra Lee Chapp

Dedication

To my daughter, Sheri, and four grandchildren, Tyler, Alexandra, Nicholaus and Gabi

Willy and the Sea Captain

Preface

Years ago while I was in California attending my aunt and uncle's golden wedding anniversary celebration, my cousin Pat Isaac made arrangements for the younger family members to see a physic. I was one of the chosen few. At the reading, the physic told me that one day I would write a book. While I was skeptical at the time, I became interested in writing full-time about the time I was ready to retire and needed something to occupy my time. So here goes my first attempt at writing. I hope you enjoy the book as much as I did writing it.

Willy and the Sea Captain

Sandra Lee Chapp

Table of Contents

Willy and the Sea Captain

Chapter 1

As the golden sun rose slowly over the slate,
steel grey mountains, and the mist swirled across tree tops and
shrouded the valley in a protective cocoon, Lady Alexandra,
road her silver-grey steed, Storm, along the ridge at a neck
breaking speed. Her groom, Jamal, had given up trying to keep
pace with her today.

Lady Alexis, as Lady Alexandra was referred to
by her close friends and acquaintances, was unusually beautiful
with a head of gilded strawberry blond curls burnished with
mahogany highlights. Her honey colored skin glistened as she
and Storm glided across the ridge. In her cinnamon velvet riding
outfit, trimmed in red fox, she was a vision of youth and
innocence.

Until this morning, she had enjoyed helping her
father, Lord Spencer, run his estate. Unlike most girls her age,
Lady Alexis had been raised as a boy since her mother died

shortly after giving birth to her. Her father didn't have any sisters and really didn't know what to do with a daughter, especially one as provocative as Lady Alexis.

Lady Alexis and her father had a very special bond. He included her in all of his outings. When she was just barely walking, he taught her to ride. She had been tutored with her brothers while she was growing up. Consequently, she was one of the few young ladies her age that could read, write and keep the estate account books. She spoke fluent English, French, and German, and could fire a pistol, duel with a sword, and was an expert markswoman with a bow and arrow.

Lady Alexis' father was Lord Spencer Hazelton Leighton, the fifth Earl of Chesterfield. Lord Spencer was a portly man with a kind heart who was loved by all who knew him. It was while Lord Spencer was at Eaton that he first met Lord Thomas Seth Craven, the fourth Earl of Thorpe. One night while the young men were out sowing their oats, the two had

10

agreed to join their families together forever by betrothing their oldest son and daughter.

As luck would have it, Lord Thomas married Lady Anne two years after the executing the betrothal agreement. A year later they had a son whom they named Lord Derek. Lord Spencer married Lady Louisa two year thereafter, but Lady Louisa did not conceive for 5 years. When she finally did conceive, their first born was son whom they christened Robert Francis Spencer Hazelton Leighton. Robert was followed by another son in two years christened Jeffrey Paul Chatham Leighton.

Lady Louisa had a difficult child birth with little Lord Jeffrey and while her doctor had advised her against bearing any more children, Lady Louisa knew how much Lord Spencer wanted a daughter to unite with Lord Thomas' son Lord Derek. So without waiting to fully regain her strength, she became pregnant again when Jeffrey was only two months old.

It was an extremely dangerous pregnancy and Lady Louisa had to be confined to bed for most of its duration. Weakened by the lack of any physical exercise, she was not strong enough to survive Lady Alexis' birth.

At Lady Alexis' christening, Lord Spencer and Lord Thomas updated the documents necessary to bind and unite their families forever. Although Lord Derek was already twelve years old when Lady Alexis was born, he showed no interest in the tiny wrinkled infant when told she was his future wife.

Lord Derek was an intelligent, as well as, impetuous child. It was obvious to Lord Thomas from a very early age that it was going to take his firm hand to prepare Lord Derek for the responsibilities that lay ahead of him.

By the time Lady Alexis was old enough to accompany her father and brother on hunting trips to the estate of Lord Thomas, Lord Derek was either away at school, traveling abroad or at sea. Consequently, Lady Alexis grew up without ever having met Lord Derek.

This morning, shortly after breakfast, Lady Alexis' father had taken her aside and given her a stern lecture on her responsibilities. He reminded her that she was well past the marrying age and would soon be past her child-bearing years. She should be thinking of her own future and not of her father and brothers. After all, Robert was betrothed to Lady Leah Byrthridge and was to be married next summer after his tour of duty with her Majesty's Service was over. Naturally, Robert would be staying on and helping his father on the estate after his marriage and should not have to be burdened with his sister.

Lady Alexis sat speechless as she watched her father pace in front of the burnt amber ledgestone fireplace with his hands folded behind his back. As a ray of morning sun filtered through the leaded glass in the study window, Lady Alexis gathered her wits and very slowly raised herself off the settee and walked over to where her father had stopped pacing, and was facing her waiting for her acceptance. Lady Alexis placed her hands on her father's shoulders and looked directly at him as she spoke, "Father, you know how much I love you. I would do anything you asked of me to please you. How could you send me to a man I do not know? A man, who if I passed him on the road, I would not recognize, a man who has made no attempt to see me all these years, who hasn't made any attempt to court me."

Lord Spencer ran his hand down the side of Lady Alexis' face, cupping her chin; he lifted her face to look at him as he tried to explain why this marriage was so important.

"My darling daughter, Lady Alexis, whom I love more than life itself, your mother sacrificed her life for you so that she could fulfill our obligation to Lord Thomas. You are a very beautiful and very special child. You need a very special man in your life. Thus far, even though you are educated and have your freedom here on the estate, you have missed so much of life and its pleasures because of my selfishness. It is because of my love for you that I am setting you free my little one. Lord Derek is a good man even if he is a little ruthless and restless. You are just what he needs to give his life peace and true happiness. You are very fortunate that he waited for you all of these years."

"But Father," Lady Alexis started to protest. Lord Spencer quickly released his hold on her. As he turned on his heel and walked to the door of his study, he called back to her, "Lady Alexis, with or without your cooperation, you will be wed this spring."

As her father spoke, Lady Alexis clinched her fists at her side and held back her temper. As soon as her father left the room, she stormed upstairs to her room tearing off her morning gown and put on one of her riding outfits. She hastened to the stables and shouted at Jamal to saddle Storm.

15

Willy and the Sea Captain

The swirling grey mist had disappeared from the ridge and the golden sun was high in the cloudless aqua sky as Lady Alexis road back towards the estate. Even though she had ridden hard for almost an hour, she was still furious with her father.

Her emerald green eyes glistened with the turmoil she felt within. How could her father suggest such a thing as marriage? After all, she was only seventeen. He had never forced her to have a season in London nor made her attend any of those silly schools of etiquette that were so fashionable among the young girls her age. Her father had always let her have her own way. Why was he forcing her into a marriage she did not desire? If she were lucky, maybe her soon to be betrothed wouldn't want her or was already secretly married.

Didn't her father say that the final arrangements had still to be made? Yes, she must think of a way to get out of this impending marriage. No man was going to make her stay home and run his house while he roamed all over the world experiencing the grandeur of the Colonies with their wild Indians and vast frontiers, or feel the salty spray of the ocean on his face and arms while she was heavy with child.

There were so many places and things she had read about and discussed with her father and brothers that she wanted to do. Now that she was finally old enough to start traveling, her father was condemning her to a life of mundane existence. Well, her betrothed was going to be sorry if he tied to force himself upon her.

She smiled at that thought. He certainly wouldn't expect her to be able to handle a knife, saber or gun, but she was considered one of the best sharp shooters around and had been besting her father and brothers since she was twelve. She was better at fencing than the fencing master her father had hired. Giorgio left quite hurriedly last year after she beat him in a fencing match and accidently tore open his arm when the tip of her foil flew off. Lady Alexis rode slowly back to the house.

While Lady Alexis was riding, Lord Spencer was sitting at his desk in his library waiting for Caldwell, his solicitor, to arrive from London. He sent for Caldwell five days ago after Robert announced his engagement. In all fairness to Robert, Lord Spencer felt it was necessary to start making plans for Lady Alexis. After all, Lord Derek was not getting any younger and Robert should not have to be burdened with his sister for life.

Lord Spencer knew that if Lady Alexis had her own way, she would never get married. He had no one to blame but himself. He had created the intelligent and independent young woman she had become by exposing her to everything his sons had. She was beautiful, but headstrong.

Her beauty was rare and he remembered how he had chased after the good looking girls when he was younger.

He didn't want just any man trying to court Lady Alexis. He chuckled to himself as the thought crossed his mind that someday she would thank him for what he had done; especially if Lord Derek was as virile as his father.

Lord Spencer recalled the last time he had seen Lord Derek. It was several years ago when Lord Derek was twenty-six. Lord Derek was a handsome well-known rake in London and was rather wealthy in his own right. He had disobeyed his father's orders five years earlier by signing aboard a frigate bound for the Colonies.

Over the years he had made several wise investment decisions and now owned his own shipping firm, five sleek vessels, and a plantation called Wynchester in the Carolinas. Although Lord Derek had made up with his parents a year ago, he still divided his time between England and the Colonies preferring to live in the Colonies.

Shortly before lunch the following day, Caldwell arrived. Caldwell had been a classmate of Lord Spencer's at Eaton and had gone on to study law.

Lord Spencer greeted Caldwell with a firm handshake. He escorted the man into the parlor for a drink before showing him to his room to freshen up and rest before dinner. Over a sniffer of brandy, Caldwell brought Lord Spencer up-to-date with the latest news from London.

After a short respite, Lord Spencer and Caldwell locked themselves in Lord Spencer's study and prepared the necessary documents activating and enforcing the betrothal agreement.

The following morning, after an early breakfast, Caldwell left for Thorpe to meet with Lord Thomas.

Chapter 2

With a rainbow of asters in canary yellow, pumpkin orange, bold red and passionate purple, and clusters of red orange bittersweet lining the stone drive leading up to the front portico of the Craven estate, Caldwell arrived at Steepleton, the estate of Lord Thomas, three days after leaving Lord Spencer's estate.

Lord Thomas had been out inspecting the new quarters being built above the stables when he heard a carriage pull in. He was surprised to hear someone approaching as he was not expecting visitors today. Most of the surrounding estates were in the middle of their fall harvesting, and the ladies were busy preparing for the approaching London winter season.

Lord Thomas was quite surprised to see Caldwell emerge from the dusty coach bearing the Leighton crest. He welcomed him with a hug and handshake and invited

Willy and the Sea Captain

him into the house. "What brings you here?" asked Lord Thomas.

"I just came from Steepleton with documents binding your family with Lord Spencer's family," replied Caldwell. "Where are my manners," replied Lord Thomas. "Metchum, show Caldwell to a guest room on the second floor so that the man can refresh himself before dinner."

So many memories rushed back to Caldwell as he followed Metchum up the winding stone stairway. He had once tutored here under Lord Thomas' grandfather, and it was Lord Thomas who had encouraged him to go on and take up the study of law. Caldwell pushed the thought aside. It had happened so long ago that it seemed like another lifetime.

After a scrumptious dinner of roast veal, partridge with mint jelly and a fresh cherry pie, Lord Thomas asked Caldwell to join him in his study for a glass of port.

Caldwell waited for his drink to be poured before he pulled out the documents Lord Spencer had given him. Handing them to Lord Thomas, he gave Lord Thomas a few minutes to scan the documents before he asked him if he remembered the agreement he had entered into with Lord Spencer when Lady Alexis was christened. Indeed, Lord Thomas had remembered his promise of long ago, and was glad Lord Spencer suggested that the two of them stop coddling their offspring and unite their two families.

Lord Thomas was delighted, but also somewhat perplexed. Lord Derek had become so independent. How was he going to break the news of his upcoming engagement to him? Of course, Lord Derek has known for years that a betrothal agreement existed, but he probably thought the whole thing had been called off by now.

Lord Thomas had seen Lady Alexis grow from a tiny wrinkled babe to the beautiful and accomplished young woman. He knew full well that she could ride and shoot, as well as, any man. He smiled as he remembered that he had forgotten to mention to Lord Derek all of these things over the years. He only he hoped he had as much luck breaking the news to Lord Derek as Lord Spencer had with Lady Alexis. Of course, Lord Derek knew he had an obligation to his family to marry a suitable young woman, and produce an heir. He was after all the next Lord.

He dismissed Caldwell for the evening and immediately sat down at his rosewood desk, picking up his quill he penned a letter to Lord Spencer informing him that he would be happy to formally announce Lord Derek and Lady Alexis' engagement as soon as Lord Spencer and Lady Alexis could travel to his estate. At that time, he and Lady Anne would host a grand ball to announce the pending nuptials.

Lord Thomas then wrote a note to Shelby, Lord Derek's cousin, asking him to come and visit immediately. He needed to convince Shelby to sail to the Colonies and bring Lord Derek home for his wedding.

Shelby reached Sussex four days after Lord Thomas sent for him. He was immediately summoned to the study by Lord Thomas, who advised him that he was needed to go to the Colonies to escort Lord Derek home for his wedding. Shelby was rather surprised that Lord Thomas felt he should go and fetch Lord Derek and escort Lord Derek back to England to get married. He surmised that Lord Derek probably didn't know about his engagement, but he agreed to go.

The Leighton household was in an uproar when word arrived by messenger acknowledging the wedding agreement and inviting all of them to travel north immediately to Steepleton.

Willy and the Sea Captain

Preparations for the trip began in earnest. A dressmaker was sent for from London to make a whole new wardrobe for Lady Alexis. Lady Alexis' maiden Aunt Sara, two score and four years old, was asked to accompany them. One of Sara's responsibilities would be to instruct Lady Alexis in the habits and ways of men so that Lady Alexis would not be shocked by what her husband would try to do to her in their marriage bed on their wedding night, and to chaperone her until her wedding. It was one thing for Lady Alexis to run free on the estate alone, but it would not be acceptable behavior for her to ride alone at Craven.

As dawn broke on the morning of the trip, Lady Alexis arrived at breakfast in her pale moss green riding outfit trimmed in ermine. Lord Spencer had trouble keeping himself from laughing as he scolded her for not dressing properly for the trip. Lady Alexis looked at him with an uplifted brow. She had

26

no idea what was so amusing as she was dressed as she always dressed for the trip north. Hadn't she always ridden Storm?

Her father promptly informed her that now that she was about to become betrothed she would be required to ride in a closed carriage with Aunt Sara; not on her horse. Lady Alexis dashed out of the room without touching her breakfast. It was obvious to Lord Spencer that Lady Alexis wasn't going to sit still and take this calmly. Lady Alexis, on the other hand, kept wondering how men, and especially her father, could make such perfect and complete fools of themselves.

It was mid-morning before Lady Alexis capitulated, changed her clothes and boarded the closed carriage with Aunt Sara.

It was a lovely November winter day when Lady Alexis and her family arrived at the Craven Estate. A light blanket of snow had fallen during the night and wrapped the grounds and building in a blanket of silvery winter fluff. A light spray of fresh salt water was blowing a gentle mist through the air like a hundred diamonds in the sky. Lady Alexis could see the white sun bleached sand at the base of the cliffs over which the carriages were passing.

Lady Alexis always felt a sense of peace and contentment at the Craven Estate as if she were coming home. Lady Anne had always treated her like her own daughter and the two women had become quite close over the years. Lady Alexis was the daughter Anne never had, and Anne was the mother Lady Alexis never knew.

There were so many questions racing though Lady Alexis' mind. What would her fiancé think of her? Would he even like her? What did he look like? What would he be like? Would he want out of this marriage as much as she did? Perhaps together they could devise a way to foil their parents' plans.

As the carriage pulled up under the front portico, Lady Alexis could see Lord Thomas and Lady Anne waiting on the veranda for them. She craned her neck as far as was lady like trying to get a glimpse of Lord Derek, but she could see no one else around.

Wasn't he the least bit curious in who she was, what she looked like, how well she could ride? After all, her father had told her that Lord Derek had only seen her once before and that was at her christening. Perhaps he was out on the estate checking on the condition of the fields or maybe he had left home when his father told him of his plans. Why the nerve of that man, not even waiting around to discuss the matter with her. Well he'd better shape up fast or she would just have to take control. Lady Alexis shook her head to clear it. What was she thinking? She wasn't going to get married. Why should she care what he thought or what he was like.

Willy and the Sea Captain

As the carriage rolled to a stop, the carriage door
was opened by Lord Thomas, and Lady Alexis was helped down
from the carriage by Lord Thomas. She threw her arms around
him and gave him an affectionate kiss on the cheek. She then
turned to greet Lady Anne; the women embraced and held each
other for several minutes. Both ladies parted with tears in their
eyes.

"Oh Lady Alexis you grow more beautiful every
day. Welcome to the family dear. You don't know how long I
have waited for this day. Come along inside now. Let me show
you to your room so that you can get refreshed."

The room Lady Alexis was shown to was done
in a kaleidoscope of blues ranging from a soft turquoise to a
shimmering royal blue. A circular down filled canopied bed
occupied most of one end of the room. The bed posts and
wardrobe were made of solid cherry wood. Two overstuffed
chairs and a chaise lounge chair were covered in chintz of pale

pink with a sliver of turquoise thread shot through it. The chairs were comfortably arranged in front of the fireplace where a few logs had been lit to take the chill out of the room. As Lady Anne was about to leave Lady Alexis to freshen up, Lady Alexis turned to her and asked, "Where's Lord Derek? Why was he not here to greet me?"

Lady Anne quickly walked across the room to where Lady Alexis was standing. She took ahold of Lady Alexis' hands and led her to the lounge chair near the fireplace. Lady Alexis felt that some of Lady Anne's initial sparkle had gone out of her eyes when she mentioned Lord Derek's name. "I hope nothing serious has happened to him," Lady Alexis said.

Lady Anne carefully explained to Lady Alexis that Lord Derek had not been at the estate or even in England when Lord Spencer's missive came. Lord Derek had been in England visiting his family late in the summer, but had left for

London to assemble his crew and head back to his plantation and business affairs in the Colonies in October.

"As soon as Caldwell brought the news from your dear father Lady Alexis, he immediately summoned Lord Derek's cousin, Shelby, and asked him to sail to Wynchester and escort Lord Derek back for the ceremony."

"I don't believe you ever met Shelby, have you my dear," remarked Lady Anne. "No, I haven't Lady Anne," replied Lady Alexis. "Well my dear, Shelby could easily pass for Lord Derek's younger brother. At 28, he was about an inch shorter than Lord Derek, and has Lord Derek's features and coloring. Shelby was the youngest son of Lord Thomas' brother, Lord Jonathon. Lord Jonathon married the only child of the Duke of Mamet and had taken over the Duke's estate when the Duke passed on several years later. He and his wife have four sons.

Lord Thomas and Lord Jonathon were very close, so we weren't surprised that the children grew to be very close. For over 20 years, Lord Derek and Shelby have always been able to confide in each other, although of late Shelby seems to have gone astray. He spends most of his time in London gambling, participating at gaming contests, drinking or picking up women. Shelby, like Lord Derek, feels he is gods' very special gift to women. He feels he has a responsibility to himself and his country not to let them down. He and Lord Derek often have contests to see who can appease the most women in one night. Oh Lady Alexis, I do hope I'm not embarrassing you by being so frank," a red faced Lady Anne said.

"No, Lady Anne, you're not embarrassing me. In fact, it pleases me to know you feel you can be honest with me."

Lady Anne squeezed Lady Alexis' hands and continued her story. "You see, Lord Thomas does indeed fear that Lord Derek will not easily give up his freedom, my dear. He felt it was necessary to send Shelby, who can be very persuasive at times, to ensure that Lord Derek returns to England for your marriage in May. Shelby complained about how expensive it was going to be to travel abroad and of the dangers he would be exposing himself to if there were pirate attacks on the high seas, as well as, the Indians he might meet in the Colonies. Shelby protested that surely someone else could go in his place, but Lord Thomas was insistent that Shelby be the one to make the journey. So with a note to Lord Thomas' banker authorizing the release of several thousand pounds and the promise of more to come when Lord Derek reached England, Shelby was off without a day's rest from his previous journey."

Lady Anne was becoming quite concerned about Lady Alexis. Lady Alexis had listened to her story with great interest, but as Lady Anne went on, Lady Alexis had slowly gotten her coloring back and then some. Lady Anne explained that problems could arise and the May wedding could be delayed if Lord Derek is at sea and not at Wynchester when Shelby arrives.

"We insisted that Shelby stay in the Colonies until Lord Derek returns. As it has worked out Lady Alexis, just yesterday we received a letter from Lord Derek advising us that he was getting ready to set sail on one of his buying trips and does not expect to be back in the Colonies until spring."

Lady Alexis was furious. How dare Lord Derek insult her by not coming back to England to meet her and talk with her? She at least had the courage to come to northern England to meet him and try to work out some sort of agreement, but how dare he not even show up to greet her. She wouldn't marry him now for all the gold in England.

Lady Anne could see the fury rising in Lady Alexis and quickly added that Lord Derek knew nothing of the pending engagement. Lady Alexis guessed she couldn't blame

Lord Derek for not showing up if he hadn't known about the engagement. Well, she would go ahead and attend the upcoming engagement ball without him.

The following morning, the fathers of the bride and groom decided to hold the engagement ball in London and then send Lady Alexis to the Colonies to wed Lord Derek. She would either meet Lord Derek upon her arrival or stay with Shelby at Lord Derek's estate if Lord Derek was at sea. They felt Lord Derek would honor the agreement once he had a chance to meet Lady Alexis and see for himself what a fine creature she was. In fact, it was probably better this way as Lord Derek would not have the chance to change his mind once Lady Alexis was there.

The servants were ordered to start packing immediately so that the families would be ready to travel the following day. Since one of Lord Derek's ships had arrived in Thorpe the day before and was anchored just of the coast, Lord

Thomas decided it would be best for both families to sail to London aboard the vessel. He sent a message on ahead to the Captain of the Santa Anna Queen asking permission for him and his guests to return to London with him. Captain McGowan wrote back granting permission for the families to sail on the morning tide with him. He suggested that they send their baggage out that evening so that the passengers could be quickly boarded in the morning and departure not delayed.

Willy and the Sea Captain

Chapter 3

Charlestown was a bustling shipping and trade center in the colonies. Ships came into port daily from all over the world. On one such ship, flying the British flag, was Shelburne Torrance Craven know as Shelby. Shelby arrived in Charlestown on a wet and windy day in early November and proceeded directly to Mistress Beth's Hotel and Eatery on Main Street to rest and change before riding out to Wynchester to meet with Lord Derek.

After a short nap, bath and dinner, Shelby decided to send a messenger with Lord Derek's parent's letter out to the plantation so that Lord Derek could digest the information before Shelby arrived to add his own personal feelings on the subject.

At Wynchester, the room was blanketed with the soft evening light. The tall, handsome broad shouldered man ran his long aristocratic fingers through his sandy blond hair. He was wearing a cream colored satin shirt open enough in the front to expose a mass of curly hair on his well-muscled chest. Years of working on ships had helped develop the powerful rippling muscles in his forearms, back and shoulders. His buckskin tan pants molded perfectly to his frame and were tucked into his freshly oiled black boots.

He was still holding the letter he had received a short while ago from his father. He kept reading and rereading it, trying to determine what had made his father demand his marriage at this time, after all, he was two score and nine.

Lord Derek and his field foreman, Garth Richards, had been going over the plantation books when the messenger arrived with Shelby's message. Lord Derek took the messages from his butler, Albert, and walked over to the French doors in his study to read them. As he read the letter, he became agitated. He had hoped his father had forgotten the betrothal agreement. He did not think his father would try and force a marriage on him at this time. Lord Derek had long ago proven that he was independent and could take care of himself.

Lord Derek turned and walked over to the fireplace where Albert had recently lit a small fire to ward off the late fall chill. An oil painting of his parents sat in a silver frame on the mantel. Lord Derek glanced up at the picture. Even though the letter didn't say so, Lord Derek felt his father must be in ill health or he would not try and force Lord Derek into something he did not want. At least not right now.

It's not as though Lord Derek would never marry and produce an heir. Why he hardly had time for a wife right now, much less think about starting a family. Marriage now would mean he would have to give up his extensive traveling. No, he wasn't ready to sacrifice all that yet; not for any woman no matter how sweet, young and innocent she is. Not that he felt Lady Alexis hadn't turned out to be a beautiful woman. His only recollection of her after all was at her christening some 17 years ago. Why she was just a skinny, mousy, little rug rat at that time. She certainly didn't appear to be a catch of any sort.

No, he was not going to bend to his father's will and demands this time; even if his father was in ill health. He was planning on sailing soon anyway and he would move up his plans to set sail for the open seas immediately and leave Shelby behind to deal with the girl.

Lord Derek knew his father well enough to know that he would send Lady Alexis to him if Lord Derek didn't return to England. Well, he would leave Shelby here to wait on the arrival of the girl. Shelby could tell them that he was on an important buying trip and that he would be in touch soon.

In the meantime, she should make herself comfortable at the plantation.

He would insist that she attend parties and balls while he was away so that she might meet the people of Charlestown. With some luck, she would find some dandy to marry her and fill her belly with his seed before Lord Derek returned. That would free Lord Derek so that he could inform his father of her unwillingness to wait for him. Yes, this would be the most logical and safest approach. He would save face with his father and retain his pride as well. Then he could take his time to find a wife.

He wondered what could have caused his parents to send a personal messenger, and especially Shelby. His father spoke very little of Shelby lately thinking he was a dandy. Only a few people outside of Lord Derek and Shelby knew that Shelby was a secret agent for the Colonies and was working undercover in England. As part of his cover, Shelby gambled and acted like a dandy. Shelby was purportedly heavily in debt again as a result of betting and losing to much of the government's money at the gaming tables. A few well-placed gold coins and the use of the plantation would provide excellent cover for Shelby's activities while Lord Derek was at sea.

Shelby could escort Lady Alexis around Charlestown until Lady Alexis had a chance to meet some of the more eligible men in town. Perhaps she and Shelby would take a liking to each other and Shelby would get her into his bed before he returned. Neither father would expect him to marry a girl who had slept with someone else. Yes, he would send for Shelby tomorrow morning and invite him to stay at the plantation. Lady Alexis was after all responsible for turning his father's ear and getting him to uphold the betrothal agreement.

The more he thought about it, the more he decided that Lady Alexis was probably a homely old maid anyway. She probably thought that a wealthy dowry could buy her a handsome husband and title. Well, he didn't need any woman's dowry. He had made more in the past ten years then his father had made in his lifetime. Since Lord Derek arrived in the Colonies, he has never asked his father for money. He felt certain Shelby would head in her direction if he let it slip that Lady Alexis was looking for a husband and was worth her weight in gold. Yes, Shelby will pursue Lady Alexis and marry her freeing him of his obligation.

The following morning, Lord Derek called for Albert and asked him to go into Charlestown to fetch his cousin, Shelby. Albert raised his eyebrows and questionably gazed at Lord Derek. Something wasn't right here. Lord Derek usually went out of his way to avoid his cousin. Perhaps the boy had a might too much of the drink. "Excuse me sir, but did you say I was to fetch Shelby from the pubs and gambling dens of Port Charleston?"

"Yes, my good man, and be quick about it. I also want you to take a message to Captain Russell. I want him to stock the ship, gather the crew, and be ready to sail at dawn tomorrow." "Isn't this a mite peculiar sir? I mean, you just docked a few days ago. You don't even have your land legs back yet, and Miss Suzanne from the Flowergate Plantation will be upset if you're not around to attend her ball. After all, she purposely postponed having the ball until you docked."

"Do as I ask and don't question me, Albert, or you'll force me to ship you back to England. Maude is still pretty anxious to get you to the alter you know." Albert turned beet red at Lord Derek's last remark. Lord Derek knew how to hit home when he wanted to. "As you say sir," Albert replied, and left the room to go and prepare for the ride into town.

It was after midnight before Albert returned with a slightly weaving Shelby. Shelby was glad to have Albert fetch him as it gave him a good excuse to leave, and also necessitated

Albert having to cover his gaming losses for the evening. Lord Derek must really have gotten himself in a mess this time to have willingly bailed him out or maybe it was the letter regarding his upcoming wedding that set him off.

Lord Derek looked up from the book he was reading when Shelby entered. He smiled, stood up and crossed the length of the room in three long strides. He grasped Shelby's hand and put his other arm around him while leading him to a chair by the fire. Lord Derek asked Albert to please bring them some tea and sandwiches. Shelby looks like he needed something substantial to clear his head.

Shelby was dressed in a peach satin suit with a beige ruffled shirt surrounded by a cummerbund of magenta silk. Shelby wished Lord Derek would be a little more conscience of his appearance. He looked so drab in his buckskin britches and shirts. Shelby sat tall with a smirk on his face waiting for Lord Derek to acknowledge him. He knew Lord Derek well enough to know that his father's message had not set well with him. "Lord Derek, how good to see you ole fellow. You're looking well."

Lord Derek immediately asked Shelby how his father and mother were.   Shelby replied, "Quite well, actually Lord Derek. In fact, as you are probably aware, I'm here at their request. They've asked me to fetch you home immediately for your wedding."

Lord Derek cocked one eyebrow at that remark. Lord Derek took a seat across from Shelby and said, "Shelby, I have a favor to ask of you. I don't know if you recall my father's best friend, Lord Thomas Leighton in England, the estate of Lord Thomas?"

"No, as a matter of fact I don't," replied Shelby. "Well, that's all right," Lord Derek said. "Lord Thomas had three children, two boys and a girl. The oldest boy is in the Queen's navy and another one is studying at Oxford. The daughter is the youngest and quite a talented and beautiful young lady I'm told."

"As you know, I haven't been home until recently, so I can't give you any firsthand information, only what my father tells me. As you may or may now know, at Lady Alexis' christening my father and her father betrothed us to each other. Since she has finally reached a marriageable age, her father and my father will be sending her to me to be married here in the Colonies if I don't return home immediately. Much to my distress, I received an urgent message this morning requiring my immediate attention. I shall have to be gone for several weeks and possibly several months. I am, therefore, seeking your help in welcoming Lady Alexis for me and making her welcome here until I can safely return home to marry her."

"She will be carrying a sizable dowry with her and will require your constant care and protection. I realize what a burden I'll be placing on your shoulders, asking you to live here until I return. Do you think you could do this for me ole boy, I can't tell you what is would mean to me to know you are here looking after her and her dowry."

The whole time Lord Derek had been talking, Shelby had to keep himself from jumping with joy. Lord Derek was giving him the answer to all of his eminent problems. He didn't feel like rushing back to England so soon after his arrival. He now had an excuse for asking for a leave of absence from government service in order to handle Lord Derek's estate. It also would help him keep his cover by giving him enough money to continue gambling. He also would be able to woo a rich heiress who purportedly had a huge dowry that would be his if he could bed her and wed her before Lord Derek returned, plus the use of Lord Derek's house for parties and such.

What a windfall, what good luck! Apparently, Lady Alexis wouldn't know Lord Derek if she passed him on the street. He would just have to pass himself off as Lord Derek long enough for her to fall madly in love with him. Then he would tell her the truth and urge her to marry him before Lord Derek returned. He tried not to think how angry Lord Thomas would be with him for changing sides. After all, a fellow had to look after one's own best interests.

He turned to look Lord Derek straight in the eye and replied, "Why Lord Derek, I would be honored to entertain your fiancée until you return. How unfortunate for you to have to be called away at a time like this. Rest assured I will protect your bride-to-be from all possible harm. We will both anxiously await your return. How soon do you think you will be leaving?" Shelby asked.

"With the morning tide," replied Lord Derek. "Well, this is rather sudden, but I'll just have to make some sacrifices and bear up under the strain for you. I owe you and I am sure you would do the same for me if our positions were reversed. If you'll show me my quarters, I'll retire for now. I'll send one of your footmen into town tomorrow to fetch my clothes and personal belongings."

Lord Derek couldn't believe it had been so easy. He thought Shelby would complain about being away from the action of the city for so long. Apparently, the gambling debts were much worse than he suspected. Oh well, it was still worth it if he could get out of this marriage. With that thought, he and Shelby shared tea with a lace of brandy and the sandwiches Albert had sent in before retiring to their respective quarters.

Willy and the Sea Captain

Chapter 4

Ten weeks later, after the holiday season, the Chestergate pulled away from the English shoreline, Lady Alexis waved to her father. While she was still determined to get out the marriage her father had arranged, she was feeling a certain exhilaration at getting a chance to go to the Colonies.

The Captain informed her that the trip would take six weeks if the weather held. Six weeks in which to devise a scheme to get her out of the marriage. Perhaps Lord Derek felt just as trapped as she did and would be agreeable to postponing the marriage, at least for a while. He was after all supposed to be quite a ladies man; maybe with a little luck someone else will have caught him by the time she got there.

Lady Alexis stayed on deck until she could no longer see England. The morning breeze had picked up and the sails were billowing westward and blowing the ship rapidly away from the coast. Although Lady Alexis was sad to leave her homeland, she was excited and looked forward to the time she would spend in the Colonies. This would be her first real trip away from home and her family. As the sun rose in the sky, the air became quite humid and Lady Alexis finally decided to go below and change into something lighter and more suitable for the ocean voyage.

Her cabin was in the aft of the ship and next to the Captain's own private room. Her father had insisted she be separated from the other travelers because of her youth and beauty, and the fact that she was carrying a large sum of money and jewelry with her.

Her room was finished with a single bed which had recently been fitted with a mattress of down feathers, and a small chest. A line had been strung across one end of the room so that she could air some of her dresses out. Lady Alexis had one port hole from which she could gaze out across the ocean. She opened the port hole to allow some fresh sea air to circulate in the small cabin and laid across her bed to enjoy the gentle breeze that swept across the room.

Aunt Sara and Caren, her personal maid, were traveling with Lady Alexis and were sharing a cabin directly across the hall from hers. Their cabin was the same size except that bunk beds had been positioned in the room instead of an oversized bed. Sara and Caren had gone directly to their cabin as soon as they boarded the ship as the motion of the ship made them green.

―――――――――

The Chestergate had been at sea for three weeks. Today the weather was rather balmy, as a heavy fog descended upon them over night, and visibility was down to 300 feet. The water was choppy and Lady Alexis was getting sick from the pitching of the ship while standing on deck. The Captain had asked all passengers to stay below until the weather cleared, but Lady Alexis felt so confined in her cabin.

Lady Alexis was holding onto the deck rail and day dreaming. She had never before been confined for so long without exercise. She longed to ride Storm through the golden green fields and along the rippling steams at home. She wished for sunshine and the chance to lie in a clover field, but most of all she missed her father and brothers. She hoped this voyage would end soon so that she could get her business with Lord Derek settled and return to England for her brother's wedding.

Lady Alexis had been on deck for no more than a few minutes when all of a sudden a ship sailing black sails and flying a crossbones flag loomed just off the ship's port bow. The Mutiny fired a cannon ball at the Chestergate and broke the top mast off half-way slowing the ship down immediately. The Captain bellowed for all passengers to go below and to lock themselves in their rooms until the ship was out of danger.

Horrified, Lady Alexis turned and fled to her cabin. She tried Aunt Sara's door and found to her relief that it was open. She sped inside and stood against the door gasping for breath. Aunt Sara and Caren were concerned about her pale countenance and asked what the ruckus was on deck.

Lady Alexis quickly told them that a pirate ship had appeared out of nowhere and had fired on the ship knocking off the top mast. The pirate ship was now bearing down on them. Aunt Sara told Lady Alexis to immediately take off her clothes while she and Caren rubbed her down with an allergy paste. Upon hearing her Aunt's words, Lady Alexis realized for the first time what could happen to them if the pirates came on board. She felt faint and collapsed to the floor of the cabin.

Sara sent Caren to find the strawberry roots in her trunk while she helped Lady Alexis to the bed. While Aunt Sara made a paste from the roots mixed with water, Caren stripped Lady Alexis' gown off her and gave her an old night shirt to put on that she brought along to make rags out of in the Colonies. Sara quickly rubbed the paste over Lady Alexis' body.

She then grabbed the lantern and poured some of the oil from its base into her hands and rubbed the oil into Lady Alexis' hair, making it clump up. Sara hoped that the pirates wouldn't stay on the ship to long so that she could clean Lady Alexis up before she blistered and scarred permanently as Lady Alexis was severely allergic to strawberries.

At that moment the door to the cabin was kicked in and several men of questionable character rushed in. Two of them already had Aunt Sara on the floor and her clothes torn from her body before Caren caught their attention hollering "pox, pox, pox" at the top of her lungs.

All action stopped at the sound of Caren's voice. Sara gathered her wits and tried to explain in a calm voice that one of the maids on the ship had come down with the pox. Since she and Caren had the pox as youngsters, they agreed to take turns caring for the maid. She quickly added that while she and Caren probably wouldn't get the pox again, that they were definitely carriers and had already spread the pox germs to the ship's crew and now them. She looked each pirate square in the eye as she asked them where or not they had ever had the pox? She then reached out and pulled the blanket from Lady Alexis, exposing a mass of ugly red blistering sores filled with puss and fluid. Some of the sores had already broken open and were oozing fluid.

The pirates slowly started backing out into the hall. Once in the hall, they turned and ran at full speed up the passageway to the deck yelling "pox on board, pox on board, abandon ship".

The pirates still on board the Chestergate dropped the goods they were transporting to their pirate ship to the deck and immediate scrambled across the gang plank to their own ship. The Mutiny started to move away. Before pulling to far way, the Mutiny fired another cannon ball at the port side of the ship and knocked a hole in the upper deck. While the ship burned, the pirate ship backed away and set sail toward the south.

As soon as the pirates left Sara's cabin, Aunt Sara told Caren to run across the hall and fetch Lady Alexis' water bowl. Sara grabbed a bar of soap and scrubbed Alexis' body down quickly. She hoped she wasn't too late in getting the paste off Alexis' lovely skin as leaving the paste on to long could cause permanent scars in the skin.

Even though she and Caren worked quickly to remove the paste, Lady Alexis had blisters over 60% of her body. Caren quickly followed up Sara's wash down with a poultice soaked in lanolin. As soon as they felt Lady Alexis was out of immediate danger, they covered her again and went up on deck to determine the extent of damage done to the ship and to see if they could help the injured crew members and passengers.

When they reached topside, they could scarcely believe their eyes. The port side of the ship was ablaze and there

Willy and the Sea Captain

were bodies of dead crew men and passengers everywhere.
They went in search of the Captain, but they could not find him.
It was obvious that they were the only passengers left alive on
the ship.

They tried to quench the fire on their own, but
were unable to stop it. It appeared they would have to abandon
ship.

They hurried back to the cabin and found Lady
Alexis stirring on her own although she was moaning and
complaining about how much she itched all over. Aunt Sara
quickly brought Lady Alexis around and explained to her what
had happened. She told Lady Alexis to put her jewelry and
dowry in as few trunks as possible while she and Caren gathered
food and water, weapons and clothes for their impending
abandonment of the ship.

As Lady Alexis ran across the hall to her own
cabin, she was thrown against the wall by a terrible jolt. As she

picked herself up and looked out the port hole, she saw a sheet of rain pelting the ship. Waves up to ten feet high and tipped in white foam were brushing up against the ship causing it to pitch violently. She pushed herself from the wall and called for Sara to stop packing and bring Caren up on deck.

Lady Alexis knew from conversations she had with the Captain that the three of them had to get the ship turned into the storm or they would capsize. She also knew that they had a better chance of surviving on this big ship then they would in a row boat in the middle of a stormy violent ocean.

Lady Alexis stopped briefly as she got top side. Although Aunt Sara had explained what had happened; she was unprepared for the devastation she saw. She shuddered to think what the pirates would have done to her if her Aunt hadn't stopped them.

When she found Sara and Caren, the three of them climbed the ladder to the upper deck where the massive steering column was located. It was going to take all of their strength working together to get the ship turned. They silently prayed that the rudder had not been damaged.

As the rain continued to pour down in thick sheets, they struggled with the wheel. As soon as they got it to budge slightly, a strong wave would hit the side of the ship causing them to fall and lose control of the wheel. Each time they lost their grips, the ship would turn again. As their strength waned, they finally got the ship turned. The trio hurriedly tied the wheel in place and went below deck.

It was a somber group that made their way toward the hold of the ship. Lady Alexis decided they should all return to their cabins and rest and pray that God would spare their lives for they had done all that they could to try and save the ship and themselves.

In her cabin, Lady Alexis quickly shed her soaked garments. She was going to have to change her style if she intended to survive this journey. All of a sudden she remembered that the Captain was about her height, although much broader and muscular. Perhaps he had something in his cabin she might wear. She hurried down the hall to the Captain's cabin and prayed the door wasn't locked. She tried the knob and the door opened.

Lady Alexis was in awe at the opulence she found within. A large double bed was in the rear of the cabin on a raised floor. Across the headboard was carved a nude of the most beautiful mermaid she had ever seen. Over the bed, in the recessed ceiling were mirrors with gold veins surrounded by painted nudes of every type woman imaginable.

She crawled up on the bed and laid across the bed to get a better look at the ceiling. Starring back at her was a Mexican lady, a Spanish lady, a French mademoiselle, an Egyptian princess, an English lass, a Russian woman, and several other women whose nationality she could not determine.

Willy and the Sea Captain

She was particularly astonished at the beauty of the maiden who had reddish blond curls like her own, burnished golden skin tone, delicate features, and small perfectly molded breasts. She didn't know much about men, other than what her Aunt told her, but the young maidens on the ceiling seemed excited at the prospect of what was going to happen to them.

She stifled a giggle as she imagined the old Captain in here with his lady friends all eagerly waiting. Waiting for what? She remembered Aunt Sara's talk with her about husband's rights.

All at once, she heard a loud thud as if another ship had come along side. A few seconds later she heard footsteps on the deck and the door leading down into the cabin area opening. Because of the mist, she couldn't quite make out the man's features that now loomed over the bed, but he was huge. When he saw her there on the bed, he smiled at her and called her his golden mermaid. She tried to tell him he was wrong, she wasn't a mermaid, but Lady Alexandra Leighton, but no words would come from her mouth as he moved towards her.

As he sat at the end of the bed, smiling down at her, she felt herself grow faint. Before she knew what was happening, he was lying there on the bed beside her, beckoning her to move into his embrace. The last thing she remembered was his golden hair, muscular chest, and the power of his arms as he embraced her.

She wasn't sure how long she slept, but Lady Alexis woke with a start as bright rays of sun poured thought the port holes. It took her a moment to realize where she was and what had transpired the day before. She had come to the Captain's cabin in search of more suitable clothing. Apparently, she had fallen asleep while gazing at the unusual ceiling. Her mystery man of the night before was gone and she realized he was only a dream, a figment of her imagination.

Willy and the Sea Captain

She quickly climbed down from the bed and walked over to the wardrobe. In it she found just what she was looking for, a pair of black pants that were much to large, but covered her legs and allowed her to move freely. She tied the top of the pants with a piece of leather she found in a desk drawer and donned one of the Captains' white frilly shirts. She gathered the shirt tails and tied them around her waist. She also found one of the Captain's hats and pushed her own long red golden hair underneath the brim. While she was at it, she donned a sword and pair of pistols. There was no way she would be able to keep the Captain's boots on so she decided to wear a pair of her own riding boots.

As she passed her Aunt's cabin, she softly opened the door and peered in. Sara and Caren were still sleeping soundly. She closed the door quietly and went up on deck to survey the damage in day light and look for some food in the galley.

The storm from the night before had washed the bodies on deck overboard along with the debris left from the bloody battle. She saw that the main top mast had been broken off about half-way up by a cannon ball. Perhaps between the three of them they could rig sails on the main mast and the lower mast. The port side of the ship was charred slightly from the fire, but wasn't listing. She walked across the deck and went below on the port side to see how much damage was there. Besides the galley was on the port side and it was the only way she could get food for herself, Sara and Caren.

Lady Alexis was once again not prepared for what confronted her below. While all signs of the raid had been washed clean on the upper deck, below she found bodies of the crew and passengers. The reality of it all finally hit her and she ran back up on deck gasping and weeping. She jumped as she felt an arm go around her waist. She turned to see Aunt Sara standing there, telling her to go ahead and cry herself out. Aunt Sara held her in her arms as she cried.

After Lady Alexis had cried herself out, Aunt Sara suggested that Lady Alexis go below and prepare breakfast while she and Caren tried to dispose of the bodies. She suggested that they take inventory after breakfast and try to read the charts to determine how far off course they were. Perhaps if they could get a few sails raised, they could head the ship towards a shipping lane and wait to be rescued.

Lady Alexis was glad to have the diversion. She tried not to look at the bodies as she made her way to the kitchen.

Fortunately, the kitchen was not damaged. She opened several of the port holes to allow air to circulate into the cabin. She found plenty of food in the storeroom. She estimated that there was enough food to last them for several months. Thank God they would not starve.

Quickly Lady Alexis prepared a breakfast of hotcakes, bacon, grits, tea and eggs. There was small oak table in the kitchen that the cook must have used to set the prepared food on while waiting for the cabin mates to deliver the filled trays to the passengers. In the bottom drawer of one of the cabinets, she found several checkered table cloths. She took one table cloth out, shook it and placed it over the table. She felt it would be best for them to take their meals here until the ship was cleared.

As soon as breakfast was ready, Lady Alexis glanced out into the passageway and was relieved to see that the bodies and been removed and the floors and walls mopped. She called out to Sara and Caren that breakfast was ready.

Aunt Sara opened the door above and shouted down that they would be there as soon as she and Caren washed up.

Lady Alexis' curiosity got the best of her and she started opening the other cabin doors in this part of the ship while waiting for Aunt Sara and Caren. She was surprised that the rooms were not private and were not as nice as the ones at her end of the ship. In one room, there were 15 to 20 hammocks stretched along each wall. It appeared to be the crew's quarters. One of the other larger rooms appeared to have been inhibited by the other passengers on board.

She opened the door at the far end of the passageway and found herself staring out into the ocean. As she stood there looking at the gaping hole that had been made by a cannon ball, she was buffeted by a mist of sea water. This was the room in which the last cannon ball had entered. The room was barren and charred. Whatever had been there had either been washed out to sea during the storm or burned. She realized that they were lucky to still be afloat.

Next to the galley she found the luggage room where many of the trunks had been torn open and clothes scattered over the floor of the room. It appeared the pirates had opened the trunks looking for gold and jewelry. Later when she had time, she would come back and sort through the luggage. Perhaps she could identify their owners. When they reached port, the belongings could be returned to the passenger's next of kin.

She heard footsteps in the hall and somberly turned back towards the kitchen. Aunt Sara and Caren were already seated at the breakfast table, serving themselves when she walked in. She took her place at the table and piled more food than she thought she was capable of eating on her plate.

Very little conversation was made over breakfast. Each of them seemed to be absorbed in their own thoughts. As Caren was pouring the last of the tea for them, Lady Alexis spoke, "How many bodies did you find?"

Aunt Sara said, "About 17 in all. Most of them trapped below deck. We also found the cook's body and several of the men who were preparing to relieve the day crew. Most of the men were either washed overboard yesterday during the storm or thrown overboard during the raid. We never found or saw the Captain's body."

"Are there any other survivors?" asked Lady Alexis.

"No, just us," Aunt Sara said. How horrid, Lady Alexis thought. If it hadn't been for her Aunt's quick thinking, she wouldn't be alive now. She got up from her chair and walked over to her Aunt's place. She gathered the woman in her arms, and told her how much she loved her and how glad she was that she had decided to accompany her. For without her, she probably wouldn't be alive now, and if she was, she wouldn't still be virgin. As much as she wanted out of her betrothal agreement, she didn't want Lord Derek to leave her because she had already been bedded by a pirate.

Aunt Sara told her she understood, but that Lady Alexis really deserved the thanks for saving all their lives and their virginity. If it hadn't been for Lady Alexis' allergies, she didn't know what she would have done.

Caren blushed when Sara referred to their purity, but she kept her mouth shut and decided not to tell them that it was a few years to late to worry about protecting her virginity.

Lady Alexis suggested that the women change while she went to look for the ocean routing charts. Caren said she wasn't about to gad about like a man, but she volunteered to clean up the kitchen while Sara and Lady Alexis looked for charts.

Lady Alexis did not want her Aunt to see the Captain's cabin, so she suggested that her Aunt survey the damage done to the main top mast and sails while she searched the Captain's cabin for charts. Lady Alexis remembered seeing several scrolls near a trunk she had opened earlier looking for something to wear. Perhaps those were the maps they were looking for.

In the Captain's cabin she found the ship's log on the Captain's desk. She quickly grabbed it and the scrolls that she saw earlier and headed back up on deck.

Upon inspection, the scrolls turned out to be the maps they needed. Lady Alexis and Sara estimated that the storm had blown them off course by approximately 10 miles. Without a main top mast, they would have trouble getting back into a main shipping lane. It appeared that their best course of action would be to continue to drift southwest until they crossed a southern shipping lane.

Lady Alexis lost no time turning the ship around so that they would be headed in the right direction.

Chapter 5

Lord Derek spotted what he thought was an abandoned ship shortly before dawn in mid-March. He told the first mate to fire a warning shot across the bow of the ship to see if there was anyone on board.

When there was no response, he ordered his crew to head for the disabled vessel. As his ship drew closer, he was able to read the name on the hull, Chestergate. If he recalled correctly, the ship was an English passenger vessel reported missing at sea several months ago. What would the ship be doing drifting this far from its route?

As the Charming Madam pulled alongside the Chestergate, Captain Berne, as Lord Derek was known to his crew, called out, "Ahoy, Captain of the Chestergate, this is Captain Berne. We request permission to board."

Willy and the Sea Captain

Lady Alexis, Sara and Caren had been in the crews quarters sorting through trunks and personal effects of the passengers when they felt the ship jolt as if it had been hit by something. As they heard the shout of Captain Berne, Lady Alexis quickly knotted her hair up on top of her head and pulled a cap down over her hair to cover her hair and part of her face. Sara and Caren quickly tore a sheet in several long pieces and bound Alexis' breasts so that it would not be apparent that she was a young female.

The three women expected the worse to happen. While they had wished to be rescued, they knew that it was far more likely that another pirate ship would find them first. When the pirates finished with them, they would either be slain or sold into bondage as indentured servants. Sara felt a responsibility to Lady Alexis' parents and told Lady Alexis to keep her mouth shut as she was going to pass her off as a young mute lad. Sara also suggested Lady Alexis remove the sword and pistol she was carrying.

Lady Alexis gave her Aunt and Caren a look that Sara knew meant trouble. "My dear Aunt, if we are to be rescued it won't really matter if I've got weapons. On the other hand, if we're being attacked, I for one intend to go down fighting." Lady Alexis's then pushed Sara and Caren aside and went out to meet their captors.

Lady Alexis cautiously moved up the stairway to the main deck. As she reached the top of the stairway, the door above her burst open and the lead pirate quickly drew back and pulled his sword. Sara and Caren screamed at the bottom of the passageway. As the pirate started to advance on her, Lady Alexis drew her own sword and charged the pirate. The man quickly dropped his sword as Lady Alexis cut his right arm to the bone on her first charge.

Before Lady Alexis had time to turn around, another pirate charged at her. Here was a man who knew how to fight. He was strong and very quick. Much quicker than her father and brothers had been. She knew that unless he slipped or made a mistake, she would have trouble beating him. Lady Alexis glanced up at the pirate and her breath caught in her throat. She had never seen such a handsome man before. He was more than a head taller than she was with the deepest blue eyes she had ever seen. He looked like a Greek god with his blond hair and muscled chest. She felt herself grow weak as she looked at him.

Captain Berne feeling her eyes upon him glanced carefully at the young lad and was surprised by the intense look he was being given. Captain Berne scowled as Lady Alexis caught him on the forearm with the tip of her sword causing a slight flesh wound. He quickly parlayed by cutting a line just under her right arm pit to her waist. She was saved from a fatal wound by the binding she had on her breasts. The pirate was caught momentarily off guard when the tip of his sword caught in her clothing.

Lady Alexis charged around to his left side and plunged her sword into his groin. The pirate let out a howl and he dropped to the deck of the ship. Before he hit the deck, he drew his knife and threw it at Lady Alexis. Lady Alexis tried to reflect the knife off her sword, but as it hit the sword it ricocheted into her right breast. Blood rapidly covered the front of her shirt as she fainted.

Rocky, the Charming Madam's doctor and first-mate, rushed forward to the Captain's side. He felt for a pulse and was relieved to see that the Captain had a strong pulse, but had apparently fainted from intense pain. He ordered several of the crew to carry the Captain and the young lad below and for the crew to haul the other two ladies over to the Charming Madam.

Willy and the Sea Captain

He immediately went below to the room where the Captain had been taken, and began to remove his clothing.

The Captain was starting to come around and was moaning, cursing profusely, and asking if he had lost his manhood forever. Rocky gave the Captain a dose of whiskey to quiet him down while he worked on him. He bathed the Captain and treated his wounds. Most of the wounds were superficial and required little care. The wound to the groin area was not serious, just painful.

As he was covering the Captain with a blanket for the night, Huey, a sailor from the other ship came running into the Captain's cabin and yelled for the doc to come over to the other cabin immediately and take a look at the lad. He was mumbling something to the effect that Rocky and the Captain weren't going to believe what happened.

Rocky rushed out and told Huey to calm down so that he could understand him. Huey pushed the door to the adjoining room aside and let Rocky in. There on the bed lay the most beautiful woman Rocky had ever seen. She was nude and her glorious strawberry curls circled her head like a halo. She was covered in blood and it took Rocky a minute to understand the implications of what was before him. The awakening hit him like a thunderbolt.

The Captain had been dueling with a woman. She was the one responsible for the pain the Captain was now suffering. Rocky doubled over with laughter as the irony of the situation hit him. The Captain was a true ladies' man and wouldn't damage a hair on this maiden's head under normal circumstances. Likewise, the lady had just about done the Captain in which wouldn't sit well with the Captain's ego.

He turned to Huey and asked him if anyone else knew that the lad dueling the Captain was really a maiden. Huey said he hadn't told anyone the truth for fear the Captain would tar and feather him for spreading rumors. Rocky suggested that he not tell any of the other crew members just yet. As for telling the Captain, well he would find out soon enough. Best to wait for the Captain's wounds to heal first.

Rocky cleaned and wrapped the maiden's wounds and told Huey to stay with her and not let her out or anyone else in. Rocky then went back on deck to talk to the other women that had been on the ship.

Sara and Caren were still on the Chestergate arguing with the crew and refusing to cross over to the Charming Madam.

Rocky walked over to where they were standing and whispered to Sara that he knew what and who the lad was. "Madam, what may I ask you are you doing out here in the middle of nowhere, alone, without any men on board, and what happened to the rest of the crew?"

Sara looked him straight in the eye as she spoke, "Sir, our ship was attacked several weeks ago by pirates. They slew our Captain and the crew. What passengers didn't jump over board were slain. Where is Lady Alexis and what do you intend to do with us?"

Rocky assured Sara that they were not pirates and that no harm would befall them. He would make the necessary arrangements to see that they were put ashore as soon as possible. He introduced himself as Captain Berne's first mate from Virginia. He asked Sara who she was and who was traveling with her. Sara introduced herself and Caren.

She stepped closer to Rocky and whispered to him that Lady Alexis really didn't mean to hurt those men; she was only trying to protect herself and them. Rocky said he understood and that their secret would be safe with him. He told her that she and Caren would have to spend the rest of the voyage on the other ship for their own safety. Sara started to protest, but Rocky assured her it was for the best, especially if the ship was attacked again before they reached port.

"With a few minor repairs, this vessel will be as good as new. With a tow line to the Charming Madam, we should be able to reach port for repairs in about six days."

Sara and Caren were transferred to the other ship and a tow line was hooked up to pull the Chestergate behind the Charming Madam. All the crew members except for Huey and Rocky were sent back to the Charming Madam for the duration of the voyage.

Rocky went below deck to check on the Captain and the maiden. He found the maiden up and pacing the floor of her cabin demanding to see the Captain. Rocky quickly told Huey to go and prepare trays for the two patients while he talked to the lady.

Rocky turned to face her as soon as Huey left. "Madam what kind of fool are you? The Captain will strangle you when he finds out what a fool you made of him in front of his crew. You do know where you stabbed him?"

Lady Alexis was furious herself. She quickly spat back, "Yes, I know darn well where I hit him and I hope he's permanently damaged. He's probably raped more women then he can count. I've performed a great service for the women of the world by taking him out of action."

"Well madam, the Captain does not know what you really are yet. If I were you, I wouldn't let him know just yet either. I suggest you get yourself dressed like a boy again and hope he doesn't decide to flog you for what you've done."

"Flog me for what I've done? Why he nearly cut my breast off. How do you think I look and feel with a permanent scar? You must know that I did not draw my sword first, that pirate did. Is this how you welcome all your guests?"

Willy and the Sea Captain

"Now lass, calm yourself. I promise ye, no harm will come your way if you behave yourself. I'm going to go in by the Captain now. I certainly hope you behave yourself."

Rocky turned and walked out of the cabin, leaving Lady Alexis alone to dress. He went straight to the Captain's cabin. He walked over to the Captain's bed and was alarmed to see that the Captain was perspiring from head to toe. He poured some water from the pitcher that Huey had brought below before and began to sponge the Captain down.

As he was working, Lady Alexis knocked gently on the door and entered. She became quite alarmed when she saw how Rocky was bathing the Captain. She stepped forward and felt the Captain's head. It was hot to the touch. He was running a fever.

She quickly ran to get some of the herbs from one of her trunks. She had packed an assortment of herbs and roots for use in the Colonies. She pulled several items out and took them back over to the small table in the cabin. Pushing aside the maps that were on the table, she started to pulverize the roots. As soon as she had them ground into a fine powder, she placed them in a cup and mixed water with them. She stirred the mixture until it was well blended.

She turned and walked quickly over to the bed where Captain Berne was sleeping. She asked Rocky to lift his head so that she could spoon some of the medicine into the Captain's mouth. As Rocky lifted the Captain's head and shoulders he moaned. Lady Alexis was able to get several spoons of the inky liquid into his mouth before Rocky had to let the Captain slide back on the bed.

Lady Alexis was once again stunned at how handsome the Captain was. She suggested to Rocky that he go and grab a bit to eat while she sat with the Captain. She assured Rocky that the Captain would sleep for several hours. Rocky was thankful for the respite, but wasn't too sure he should leave the girl with his Captain. What if she decided to finish him off? Lady Alexis saw the concern in his eyes and quickly assured Rocky that she would not intentionally harm the Captain. Rocky turned and walked quietly from the room.

Lady Alexis climbed up on the bed and sat next to the Captain. She reached over and pulled the cloth from his head. While he was still warm to the touch, the Captain had cooled somewhat since she had given him her special medicine. She rinsed the cloth in cool water and returned it to his head. She ran her hand down the side of his face and through the furrow of hair on his chest. He seemed so innocent. His features had softened considerably in sleep. She wondered how it would feel to have him hold her in the curve of his arm and to see him smile at her. The thought made her shudder.

In his delirium, the Captain stirred and reached out and knocked her hat off sending her strawberry curls flying. Instinctively he pulled her head to his chest and stroked her hair and the side of her face. He lapsed back into a deep sleep pinning her to him. She dared not move for fear he would awaken and realize who she was. Exhausted as she was, Lady Alexis soon feel asleep in his arms.

It was dawn before Rocky shook Lady Alexis awake and motioned for her to leave the room. He helped her untangle herself from the Captain. Lady Alexis had no sooner left the room when the Captain stirred. The Captain tried to get up but was hit by a wave of dizziness. Rocky pushed his head back down on the pillow and told the Captain that everything was under control and that he should rest. The Captain started to protest but was quickly silenced whey Rocky started to remove his bandages to check his wounds. The pain was intense as Rocky pulled back the bandages exposing the wound on his arm and the one in his groin area.

Rocky assured him that if infection did not set in; he would be up and about in a few days. It was then that the

Willy and the Sea Captain

Captain asked Rocky what the crew had done with the body of the cur that had cut him open. Rocky stepped back away from the bed with a shocked expression on his face. "But, but, but....Captain, the lad was only defending himself from pirates. Surely you didn't mean for him to be flogged and thrown overboard?"

The Captain responded by saying, "No man who ever hoped to be spared would have struck him below the belt." Before Rocky could respond, the Captain changed the subject, "Who was that young maiden yesterday who attended me?"

Rocky had trouble covering his surprised expression. He didn't think the Captain had seen Lady Alexis in his delirium. "What lass you be referring to Captain? There's no one but Huey, the lad and myself left on this ship. All the others were sent over to the other ship yesterday shortly after we boarded. You must have been dreaming."

Sandra Lee Chapp

The Captain agreed. The fever must have made him think and see things that were not real, especially a girl as beautiful as the one he had dreamed of. The girl was so real though. So real that he actually thought he had run his hands through her hair of copper.

Willy and the Sea Captain

Chapter 6

It took the Charming Madam six days to reach the Port of Charlestown. Sara spent the time fretting. She was so worried about Lady Alexis and Captain Berne. While he had rescued them from an unsure fate and he was extraordinarily handsome, he looked at Lady Alexis with ice cold piercing sea blue eyes, and Sara was sure he knew Lady Alexis' secret. What if Captain Berne did find out Lady Alexis' secret? How would Sara explain the Captain to Lord Derek if the Captain deflowered Lady Alexis as was sure to happen once he realized who she was?

The ships were only three days from Charlestown when a storm came upon them unexpectedly from the south. Sara was instructed to tie herself to her bed and not move around her cabin or to come up on deck until the raging gale had passed. The ship rocked and the timbers creaked under the heave-ho of the bow. The first mate had turned the bow of the ship into the wind in an effort to keep the ship from capsizing.

When the pink filled sky of dawn finally broke and the grey mist lifted, the Chestergate was no longer being towed by the Charming Madam. Sara was frantic with worry. The crew explained to Sara that they had no choice but to cut the other ship loose during storm or risk losing both vessels. They assured her that Captain Berne was the very best there was at guiding a ship through a storm and that if anyone could save the other ship it would be him.

Sara had decided that she would postpone telling Lord Derek what happened. Whether Lord Derek would agree to marriage or not wasn't going to be helped by Lady Alexis having been attacked twice by pirate ships. She would explain that Lady Alexis had taken ill shortly after leaving England and had to return to England for medical treatment. That would give Lord Derek no real cause for concern and would allow Lady

Alexis an opportunity to get word to her at Wynchester as to her location. Sara could then send for her and let her know that their secret was still safe with her.

She set her mind to this plan, and towards mid-day when the golden sun finally appeared and warmed up the sky to erase all traces of the storm, she watched as one of the mates shimmied up the mast to see if any other ships were in the area or signaling for help. As Sara watched the mate scan the sea, she silently prayed for Lady Alexis and Captain Berne's safety.

Because strong tail winds built up during the storm, the mate advised Sara that they would reach Charlestown shortly before sun-up the following day. Although Sara didn't feel as overjoyed as she once was about her trip to the Colonies, she decided to try and make the best of it and should dress in a fashion appropriate for a woman of her station.

As she went through her trunks, she realized with a start that all but one of the trunks in her cabin were Lady Alexis'. Although Lady Alexis had beautiful garments and dresses, fashions that any girl would be happy to wear, Sara was not sure that they would fit her. It had been years since Sara had indulged herself in a frilly dress. She was glad that Lady Alexis was more sophisticated than most girls her age.

As she sorted through Lady Alexis' dresses, she finally found a pale green fawn chiffon dress with a lavender underskirt to wear. The neckline had been cut quite low as Lady Alexis had not intended to wear the gown until after her marriage. Crystal beads in yellow and pink had been sewn into the skirt of the dress. She had to let the seams of the bodice out in order to squeeze into the dress as was endowed with fuller breasts. She was able to wear the slippers Lady Alexis had dyed misty lavender to match the underskirt.

She started to pull her hair back into a tight chignon, as she normally wore it, when it occurred to her that the style was not as popular in the Colonies. She decided to pull her hair back loosely and tie it with a green satin ribbon. Since her hair was naturally curly like Lady Alexis', she was able to twist her hair into large curls. As she gazed into the small hand mirror, she was startled to see how much younger and more like Lady Alexis she looked with her hair this way.

The following morning as the shoreline came into view, Sara felt as if she were coming home. A certain peace settled over her. Since the Chestergate was several weeks overdue and she was arriving on the Charming Madam, Sara knew that no one would be there to meet the ship. She knew she would have to send word to Lord Derek to let him know of her safe arrival and Lady Alexis' delay.

She was quite surprised at the developed city that greeted her and the number of ships in the harbor. It was obviously a bustling trade center. In the distance, she could see a local farmers market with what seemed like an endless supply of wares and food just waiting to be sampled.

As the plank was lowered, Sara walked off the ship with a new allure and confidence about her. She was surprised and pleased even though she blushed profusely at the number of men who openly stared at her.

Sara strolled across the cobblestone wharf to where several public carriages waited. She hailed the first carriage and asked the driver to secure her trunks and deliver them to the finest hotel in town. The driver wasn't about to object when he had such a delectable woman trying to hire him. In addition, she had the look, grace and air of landed gentry. He felt certain he would earn a gold coin for his troubles.

The Dover was the newest and most modern hotel in Charlestown. It was situated along an avenue laced with colorful pansies and bright marigolds. The scent of wild bluebells touched her senses from the wooded glen located directly behind the hotel. She alighted from the carriage and went into the hotel to register.

As Sara entered the French doors to the hotel lobby, she was astonished at the modern fixtures and tasteful details of the furnishings. As she approached the desk, in her nervousness, she dropped Lady Alexis' handbag and dropped several of Alexis' calling cards. The proprietor of the hotel quickly came to her assistance and gathered the contents of her purse. He handed the items to her and welcomed her as Lady Alexandra Leighton.

She thanked him for his assistance and debated whether or not she should correct him. For some strange reason, she decided not to. She completed registering and ordered a bath to be drawn for her immediately. The manager himself offered to show her to her room. She crossed the pink marbled terrazzo lobby floor barely noticing the soft maple blue floral carpets, brass and crystal chandeliers and tan leather furniture. Sara followed the manager up the stairs. Once in her room she quickly changed for her bath.

Consequently, the news of the lovely Lady Alexis' arrival spread quickly though out the town and surrounding countryside of Charlestown. Invitation to teas and parties soon began coming into the hotel for Lady Alexis. It seemed everyone in town was anxious to get a look at Lord Derek's fiancée. Unknown to Sara, Shelby had spread the word of Lord Derek's engagement as soon as Lord Derek's ship left port.

Seeing all the invitations piling up, Sara was at a loss as how to explain the mix-up. She suddenly realized what she had gotten herself into by not being honest with the hotel manager from the start. She needed time to sort things out. So much had happened in the past few months, being asked to be Lady Alexis' official chaperone, the trip to Steepleton, the engagement ball in London, the holiday season in London, the trip aboard the Chestergate, an attack by blood thirsty pirates, a rescue by the charming Madam, Lady Alexis dueling with Captain Berne, the storm which forced the Chestergate to be cut loose from the Charming Madam, and finally her arrival in the Colonies. She might be able to fool everyone for a while, but sooner or later the truth would come out.

Chapter 7

Lady Alexis woke with a start. She was surprised to see the flaming golden sun high in the crystal clear blue sky. A light mist engulfed the entire ship. She was still a little queasy from the pitching of the ship caused by the violent storm that broke the afternoon before. Captain Berne ordered Willy and Rocky to tie themselves to their bunks below deck shortly before the storm hit and sent Huey back to the other ship.

Since the Captain's recovery, Willy, as the Captain called Lady Alexis had been ordered to be the Captain's cabin boy. Rocky had explained to the Captain that the lad could not speak but understood verbal orders. Since the Captain needed a new cabin boy until they reached port, and the Captain also wanted to punish Willy for slicing him with his sword, Willy was chosen for the task.

One of Willy's first duties was to help Rocky hoist-up the smaller sails. Lady Alexis was about to protest when Rocky reminded her that she wasn't supposed to be able to talk. Willy boldly lifted her chin and walked forward to the rope where Rocky was pulling himself up in order to reach the lower sails. As Lady Alexis pulled herself up onto the rope and had climbed about 30 feet, she glanced down at the rushing sea below and lost her balance. She let out a cry as she made one last effort to grab the line to catch herself from falling into the rushing waters.

Captain Berne saw Willy fall. He reacted quickly; pulling off his boots, tossing his sword and knife on the deck of the ship and dove in after the lad. Rocky grabbed ropes and hurled them into the whirling water below so that the Captain would have something to hold onto when he reached the surface with Willy.

Willy hit her head on the side of the ship as she fell, stunning her. She felt herself go under, but was powerless to do anything about it. As the impact of the cold water hit her,

102

she began to struggle and gasp for air. Just as she kicked her feet and prepared to bring herself around, Captain Berne grabbed her around the waist pulling her close to his own body.

Captain Berne was caught off guard at the smallness of Willy's waist and his body's reaction to the boy. He didn't ponder the perplexing question to long as he needed to get Willy to safety first. As Captain Berne broke the surface of the water with Willy in hand, Rocky helped pull him and Willy in. The Captain waved Rocky back and grabbed ahold of the rope ladder on the side of the Chestergate and lifted Willy up over his shoulder for the climb back on board.

When he reached the deck, he called for Rocky to meet him in the Captain's cabin. Captain Berne took Willy to the Captain's quarters. He very gently laid Willy on the large bed and pulled off Willy's wet clothes. Rocky tried to stop the Captain from taking off her clothes, insisting he would take care of the lad, but the Captain pushed him aside and continued undressing Willy.

When Captain Berne took off Willy's shirt he was surprised to see Willy's chest bound. The thought that Willy wasn't Willy suddenly came to mind. That would explain why Willy hadn't been strong enough to pull himself up on the rope.

Captain Berne reached out and pulled off the lad's cap, he was shocked to see how long Willy's hair was and especially the strawberry color. Why Willy looked exactly like the maiden he had dreamed of while recovering from the sword wounds Willy had inflicted on him when they first met. Captain Berne decided to settle Willy's sex very quickly by pulling the lad's britches off.

"Well, I'll be darn, Captain. How about that. Willy's not a Willy after all," said Rocky with the best shocked expression he could conger up.

104

"Just how long have you known about this Rocky? Probably from the start. How many other people know, and why didn't you tell me? Better yet, why did Willy go around masquerading as a lad?"

"Well, Captain you can't blame Willy for the deception now. After all, the ship had already been attacked by pirates once before. I'm sure she and her aunt were just trying to protect themselves from further harm."

Willy moaned and the Captain quickly changed the subject. "How bad is she?"

"I don't know Captain," stammered Rocky. "I need to check her first. Why don't you go and get some hot water so we can clean her up as soon as I have a chance to look her over."

"Okay," said the Captain as he slowly backed out of the room. Who was she and why had she and Rocky lied to him, wondered Captain Berne. He knew Rocky's story was only the half of it. Sooner or later he would get the truth from one or both of them.

Captain Berne came back carrying a large pail of hot water and clean fresh linens. Rocky assured him that Willy only had a mild concussion and would be back on her feet within a few days.

The Captain dismissed Rocky and ordered him back on deck to work the sails. He sat with Willy for several hours, sponging the sweat off of her body throughout the morning and mid-afternoon. As dusk set in the Captain pulled the covers off of Willy to bathe her. It was then he got his first good look at her. Captain Berne hadn't realized Rocky had removed the binding from Willy's chest so that her firm breasts were now clearly exposed.

He ran his finger gently down the scar on her right breast and flinched as he remembered how he had been the one to inflict the wound on her body.

He was surprised and amazed at her strength, especially her ability to yield a sword. He felt a shooting pain in his groin and arm when he thought about her ability to yield a sword. Was she really only trying to defend herself from another pirate attack? That would account for the reason she came out of the hold swinging. And how did she manage to survive a pirate attack? She obviously couldn't be a virgin anymore. He definitely had a lot of questions that needed answering, and since she was already here, he intended to make the most of her during her captivity. He thought it rather strange that she would hide from him. Most women were genuinely attracted to him and went out of their way to be with him.

Lady Alexis awakened feeling much better. She could feel a soothing touch wash her body down. As she opened her eyes, she became quite alarmed. She realized the Captain was touching her and that she no longer had any clothes on. She quickly rolled over pulling the sheet with her. As she turned, she was hit by a wave of nausea and dizziness.

The Captain leaned back against the bed post and laughed. He then leaned across the bed and brushed her hair aside as he kissed her first on the forehead and then gently on her lips. As soon as Lady Alexis felt his touch, she braced herself to fight back. The Captain continued stroking her hair and kissing her lightly. At last she cried out, "Stop this you beast. Rocky promised to protect me from you. I swear I'll cut you in two before the day is out if you don't take your hands off me."

Captain Berne only laughed at her. He quickly pinned her hands to the bed while he rolled her over to face him. He pinned her legs to the bed by throwing his leg over the lower part of her body. He asked her very softly who she was and why had she lied to him, and reminded her not to play coy with him anymore because she obviously wasn't a virgin anymore.

Lady Alexis found it very difficult to think with the Captain so close to her. She could feel his breath on her neck without even looking up at him. Her whole body tingled from the closeness.

She could feel the hair on his chest against the top of her breasts. It was a new and tantalizing feeling for her and she didn't know quite what to do about it.

Captain Berne finally lifted her chin so that she had to look at him. "Who are you?" he asked softly.

Lady Alexis' voice caught in her throat as she gazed into his eyes. She was drowning in their murky depths. Her body started to relax. "I...., I'm....Willamena Hunter," she stammered. "I'm called Willy for short. What are you going to do with me?"

With that question, Captain Berne could no longer control his passion. He could feel the tension starting to build in her body. He lowered his mouth to hers and gently probed her mouth with the tip of his tongue. Willy found herself responding to these new feelings he was awakening in her. How could her body betray her so, she wondered.

Unconsciously she arched her body to draw him in closer. He lifted his head and bent to blaze a trail of hot kisses over her. Willy lay moaning. She wrapped her hands about his head and was pulling him to her, trying to hold onto him.

As he moved his mouth down the flat surface of her stomach, her senses returned to her. She rolled away from him so fast that Captain Berne fell off the bed and onto the floor. Losing no time, Willy scampered off the bed and grabbed one of the swords hanging on the wall.

Before Captain Berne realized what was happening, Willy was standing over him with the sword firmly pressed against his chest directly over his heart. She had exerted enough pressure on the sword to draw a trickle of blood. He had no doubt she would plunge it in him given the slightest provocation.

Captain Berne knew he was at her mercy. He asked her "What's wrong? Need I remind you that you have been more than willing to accept my advances?" As he gave her a quizzical look, Willy was hit by another wave of nausea. She dropped the sword in an effort to reach the bed to keep herself from falling to the floor. Captain Berne forgot his own safety and reached for her before she fell. He lifted her gently into his arms and placed her on the bed. He reached down and pulled the covers up over her and gently kissed her on the check as he turned and walked from the cabin. Willy was sound asleep before Captain Berne reached the cabin door.

Since that day, Captain Berne had stayed away from the Captain's cabin and had let Rocky tend to the girl. It

Willy and the Sea Captain

was on her first day back on deck, almost a week later, when a new storm came upon them.

Willy had awakened that morning feeling better than she had all week. She opened the port hole and was greeted by a warm breeze. She sensed that the vessel was not moving as fast as it had the previous day so she decided to get dressed and go up on deck to see what was going on. As Rocky had advised her, she was only to leave the cabin dressed like a boy. The Captain was somewhat leery of her. Women on board a ship were bad luck.

When Willy went up on deck, she was surprised to see the sea in all directions. She went in search of Rocky or the Captain when she collided with Rocky on the upper deck.

"Well good morning' Willy. Beautiful day isn't it? Did you have any trouble sleeping?"

"Rocky, what happened to the other ship? Did they go down in the storm? Shouldn't someone tell the Captain?"

"Don't you remember we had to cut her loose during the last storm?" If we hadn't, we'd both have capsized and sank. I'm sure the ship is safe and back in Charlestown. If we made it, she did too. Don't be fretting'."

"How is Captain Berne?" asked Willy.

"One tired Captain he is madam. I imagine' he wouldn't mind if you went below to check on him. He'll probably sleep most of today, seeing' how he was up all night."

Willy lowered her eyes so that Rocky couldn't see how she felt as she answered in a soft whisper, "No, that's fine. I just thought that maybe he fell overboard during the night."

"Oh, no Willy, the Captain is fine. You mightn't be taken' a liking' to him now would you?"

Willy flushed bright red. She spun on her heel and headed for the kitchen. She called back to Rocky over her shoulder, "How about some breakfast?"

"Sounds fine to me."

Willy went below to the galley to prepare breakfast for Rocky and herself. She was feeling apprehensive. Ever since she had pulled a sword on the Captain again, he had been avoiding her. Yesterday was the first time she had seen him since then. All he did was yell at her to go below and stay there until the storm passed. Did he not intend to talk to her again?

She couldn't help but blush with pleasure as she remembered the feel of his hands on her body, and the soft kisses he reined upon her. Would it have been that bad if she hadn't stopped him? Stopped him from what? She wasn't quite sure. All she knew is that she lost control over her emotions when he was so near. Perhaps she wouldn't stop him the next time. Oh, that was foolish thinking. A man as old as he was and as good looking, probably had a girl in every port, a wife and a house full of children. She must remember to ask Rocky about it.

When Rocky come below for breakfast, Willy had a chance to sit and talk with him. Handing him a cup of freshly brewed coffee, she said, "Rocky, how well do you know Captain Berne's wife?"

"Wife, what wife? The Captain, to the best of my knowledge has never taken' a wife. Of course, he is pretty secretive about his personal life. I don't think anyone knows where he stays when he's in the Colonies. I know he doesn't have a wife on his island."

"What island?" asked Willy.

"Oh, I really shouldn't discuss the Captain's personal life with you Willy. I'm sure if you asked him he would tell you." Willy was blushing with embarrassment and couldn't hide it.

Mid-day Rocky spotted an island off the starboard side and called down, "Land ahead Captain".

There was a plush green island up ahead. The Captain asked him to fire a cannon shot off to see if the island was inhabited. He slid back down to the deck and loaded one of the cannons. He fired the cannon and then hurried back up the mast to see if anyone from the island responded. When no one did, he decided to drop anchor and row ashore.

As he was lowering a boat, Willy came running up on deck. "Well now, Willy. What's your hurry?" asked Rocky. "I heard a shot and thought we were being fired upon."

Rocky quickly explained why he had fired the shot. Willy begged Rocky to let her come with him to scout the island. Rocky capitulated and agreed to take her along. They jumped into the row boat and started rowing.

As soon as they reached the beach, they stepped out of the boat and pulled it on shore.

The island was a lush green paradise. Peacocks, turkeys, rabbits and birds of several species squawked and fluttered to safety as the intruders reached shore.

Rocky decided to split up. They each would explore the island from a different direction. Willy was told to stay on the beach in sight of the ship in case the Captain decided to look for them.

No sooner had Rocky taken off when Willy spotted a turkey caught in the underbrush. She could smell the turkey roasting already. She quickly pulled the knife from her pants and started stalking the bird. It wasn't too long before she had the turkey by its neck. Holding its head down on a rock, she cut off its head. She tied the bird upside down on a tree branch to drain while she went looking for fruit and roots to add to the meal she was planning.

It didn't take her long to find fresh pineapples, oranges, and lemons. She also found sweet potatoes, mushrooms and carrots growing wild in a small glen. As she was about to turn around and head back to check on her turkey, she spied a hidden pool with a waterfall cascading down one end.

The pool was almost completely hidden by tall grass. Oh, what she wouldn't do for a bath, but she hadn't brought any soap with her. Perhaps she could hurry back to the ship and collect a change of clothes and a bar of soap before it got late in the day. She could pick up some flour and spices for the turkey.

She hurried back to the beach to see Rocky coming back with an arm full of tobacco. She was so excited; she had trouble explaining to Rocky that she had killed a turkey for dinner and that she need supplies from the ship to complete the meal. "Do you think we could go back and pick up some things?" she asked.

"Oh, I recon' we could," said Rocky. "In fact, I can go back and pick up what you need and bring the Captain back with me."

"Oh no, I must go and select the items myself," said Willy. She didn't want to tell him about the pool and her need for soap and a change of clothes.

"I guess you been' a woman and all, you would know better than me would what's needed. Okay, lets shove off."

"Oh, thank you Rocky. I'll fix the best meal ever, I promise."

When they reached the ship, Rocky went on board with Willy to help her carry back the supplies she needed for tonight's feast. Willy headed for the galley first, quickly packing several items she needed. She asked Rocky to go ahead and put the supplies on board the rowboat while she got some of her roots and spices from her cabin for flavoring.

She quietly went below to her cabin which was next to the Captain's cabin. She slid into her cabin and opened up the trunk containing her roots and another one containing the change of clothes that she wanted. She threw the roots, soap and the change of clothes into a sack and hurried back to the row boat.

Rocky offered to row Willy to shore and then come back for the Captain. Rocky assured Willy that it was

Sandra Lee Chapp

okay for her to stay on the island alone since there was no one else on the island.

Willy was left on the island until dusk when Rocky agreed to be back. Willy asked him if he thought the Captain would mind if they had dinner on the island. She explained that she had been at sea for so long that she thought it would be nice to eat ashore.

Rocky agreed and said he would bring a table cloth back later in the day along with some plates and eating utensils.

As soon as Willy was left alone on the island, she hurried to build a fire to roast the bird. She cleaned the turkey, made her dressing and placed the bird on a spit to cook. She then hurried to the waterfall to enjoy her bath before it got to dark and the men returned.

She stripped off her clothes and plunged into the refreshing spring water. She felt exhilarated. She swam for a while and then retrieved her soap and washed her hair. After rinsing her hair, she bathed and climbed out on a rock to lie in the sun and dry.

Several times during the course of the afternoon she checked on the turkey. It was slowly browning and the aroma filled the whole island. She wrapped several large yams she had dug up earlier and pushed them into the hot coals. She made some biscuits and placed them in a closed tin on top of the hot coals. She cleaned the fruit she had picked earlier and couldn't resist eating one of the oranges and part of a juicy pineapple. She made a lemon drink with a pitcher of water from the spring and added to it a bottle of white wine she had taken from the ship's storeroom.

When her hair was fully dried, she brushed it until it glistened. She dressed in the fresh clothes she brought with her. The dress was a bright yellow taffeta with an overskirt of blue birds and doves. She pulled her hair back and tied it with a bright yellow ribbon.

When dinner was ready, she decided to start carrying it to the beach so that the crew would not have to wait to eat. As she was digging out the yams, she could sense someone behind her. She recognized Captain Berne's scent. A slight smile came to her lips as she decided to ignore him and wait for him to acknowledge her.

Captain Berne had arrived at the island just a short while ago. He told Rocky to give him 30 minutes alone on the island with Willy before he joined them. He had a few things to discuss with Willy.

Rocky was beaming from ear to ear as the Captain left the ship. What would Willy think of the Captain since he had shaved and changed his clothes? It appeared it was going to be an interesting evening.

Willy and the Sea Captain

As Willy was pulling out the third yam from the hot coals, Captain Berne bent down behind her and reached around her and placed his hands on the sticks she was using to pull the yams out with. She pretended to be startled by his move and fell backwards into his arms.

As she looked up into his smoldering eyes, he moved his hands slowly up her arms touching her ever so softly. He took her by the shoulders and bent his head forward to kiss her fully on the lips. The tenderness of the kiss startled both of them. They had been avoiding each other since the day Willy got hurt.

The Captain felt Willy give up to the sensations and melt in his arms. He kissed her again, this time with an urgent and fiery intensity that left both of them breathless. Neither one could say anything as the Captain slowly lifted his hooded eyes to meet hers.

"You look lovely tonight Willy. I can't believe how many times I have looked at you the past several weeks and did not see through your disguise. Why? Why would anyone as lovely as you be floating on a ship in the middle of the ocean unattended? How did you learn to handle a sword? Who are you really? How could your parents send you off without a man to protect you or are you already married?"

Willy stifled a giggle. "Slow down my Captain. I can only answer one question at a time." She pulled herself from his embrace and sat up turning towards him. "First, thank you for the compliment on my beauty. You're looking rather fine yourself this evening. Were you expecting company? As to why the disguise, that should be obvious. We were attacked by pirates. If it hadn't been for Aunt Sara's quick thinking, we'd all be dead or have been sold into bondage by now. You see I am severely allergic to strawberries and have been since I was a babe. My Aunt knew this. So when the pirate ship was spotted,

Willy and the Sea Captain

Aunt Sara had me change clothes while she mixed some roots into a paste and rubbed it all over me."

"You should have seen me; I was quite a sight to behold, blistered all over. As the pirates entered our cabin, Caren hollered out pox, pox. As you can imagine, the pirates left our cabin fast. Unfortunately, it was too late for the rest of the passengers and crew."

"As to being unattended, my parents recently died over in England. It was their dying wish that I come to the Colonies to carry on the family business." She lowered her gaze as she thought of her father and brothers. She hoped they wouldn't mind her telling a lie if it saved their reputations.

Before Captain Berne could ask more questions, Willy rose and turned back towards the cook fire. "You'll have to excuse me Captain, our dinner is almost ready. If you don't mind, why don't you pull the bird off the spit and carry it out to the beach. I've laid a table cloth on the beach for us to sit on. I'll follow shortly with the yams and fruit."

"Bossy little mermaid aren't you," said Captain Berne mockingly. He picked up the spit and placed the bird on the carving board. He grabbed one of the towels she brought with her and picked up the tin of biscuits.

Willy quickly grabbed the remaining sweet potatoes from the coals and picked up the basket of fruit. She retrieved the pitcher of lemon drink from the stream and carried it to the beach.

Rocky was just pulling in as Willy stepped from the path in the woods. Captain Berne was already seated on the table cloth and was busy carving the turnkey. The air was filled with the smell of good food.

Willy quickly set the rest of the food out on the cloth while Rocky set out plates and eating utensils. Willy asked

Rocky to pour their drinks in some silver goblets she brought from the ship earlier.

The Captain proposed a toast, "To the health and happiness of our golden mermaid. May she be blessed with many children and a husband who will appreciate all of her fine qualities."

Willy blushed as the Captain made his toast. Willy asked to make the next toast. Rocky filled their glasses again and Willy said, "To all men everywhere, may they always respect the women entrusted to their care." As she raised her glass, she looked Captain Berne straight in the eye. After that she asked Captain Berne to please take some turkey and pass the plate around.

The dinner conversation was light and cheery. The men had not had a meal such as this since they left Charlestown. Willy had to admit that she hadn't eaten this well since she left London.

After the meal was over, Rocky played his harmonica while Captain Berne sang a few songs. Willy danced and whirled in the sand while Captain Berne sat back against a tree watching Willy's every move. The grace with which she moved astounded him. If only he know her secret. He somehow knew that she was not telling him the truth about herself. What was she hiding? He knew he had fallen in love with her at first sight. First sight as a woman that is. He chuckled as he recalled how it bothered him when she used to stare at him when she was parading as a lad and how he had felt an attraction to the boy.

Finally, he rose and walked over to where Willy was moving as if in a trance. He pulled her into his arms and held her close. She didn't fight him, but rather laid her head gently on his chest as he pulled her closer to him. Together they glided across the sandy beach each lost in their own thoughts. They could hear the waves breaking on the rocks near the west end of the shore and the gentle cooing of the sea gulls. When the music stopped playing neither of them were aware of it.

Rocky interrupted their dream by tapping the Captain on the shoulder. "Captain, I think we'd best be getting' back to the ship. We wouldn't want to get caught here on the island if a storm came up."

"You're right Rocky," said the Captain. "Tomorrow's another day and we shall spend some time here before continuing our journey."

As the Captain escorted Willy back to the ship, Rocky loaded the leftover food and utensils into their boat and started the short journey back to the ship giving Willy and the Captain time to linger on the ship's deck before they returned to their cabins.

Chapter 8

The early spring lilac and magnolia scented breeze was blowing gently through the willow trees lining the mossy banks of Wynn Lake, a tributary backwash of the Mississippi River. The gently sloping blue-green lawns were filled with newly blooming crocus. Off to the north, just over the ridge, the main compound of the Wynchester Plantation could be seen. The main house was built three years ago to Lord Derek's specifications. The U-shaped house rose three stories high and contained fifteen rooms in addition to servant's quarters on the third floor. A cupola had been erected on the eastern end of the house so that Lord Derek could monitor the weather and river traffic.

Sara was in awe of the sight before her as the flatboat she was riding on pulled into the landing just below the house. She had chosen to wear a pale pink lawn dress with a square neckline and bouffant sleeves trimmed in seed pearls. A ribbon of darker pink was woven into a pattern at the gathered waist and around the hem. She wore white lace gloves and carried a parasol of white and pink silk.

Shelby sent for Sara when he received word that Lady Alexis had been rescued and had arrived in Charlestown two days ago. His first inclination had been to race into town and sweep her off her feet. He was anxious to find out what had happened. He decided it might be wiser for him to let her have a few days to rest. After all, she would need her strength for the number of parties that he had organized in her honor. He penned a note to her which he asked one of the servants to deliver. The note he sent to her said:

"My dear Lady Alexandra, I was overjoyed to hear of your safe arrival in Charlestown. After a few days' rest, I will send my river barge for you to bring you safely to Wynchester where you can tell me of your travels and adventures. Your devoted servant, Lord Derek."

When Sara received the message, she sighed a breath of relief as it gave her several more days in which to decide how to tell Lord Derek of Lady Alexis' disappearance and recapture by another pirate ship. She silently prayed that Lady Alexis was well and safe.

She wished her problem could be solved as easily as Caren's had been. Caren had taken a liking to one of the mates on the Charming Madam and had asked Sara's permission to wed. Sara had willingly given it as she felt Caren deserved some happiness after what she had been through.

Sara spent the next two days walking the streets of Charlestown, visiting the shops along the way and making several small purchases. She still had not written to Lord Spencer as she really didn't know what to tell him. It would break his heart to know that Lady Alexis had not arrived and was still lost at sea.

On the morning of her trip to Wynchester, she dressed very carefully. She decided to tell Lord Derek the truth and ask for his help in writing to Lord Spencer and organizing a search party for Lady Alexis. She knew the longer Lady Alexis and Captain Berne remained together, the more likely the Captain would find out who she was.

All of her good intentions were forgotten when she walked into the study at Wynchester and saw Lord Derek. Trying to catch her breath, she looked around her. The study walls were lined from the floor to the ceiling with books on every imaginable topic and in seven different languages. She assumed Lord Derek had collated them on his adventures throughout the world.

The south wall facing the front of the house was lined with windows from the floor to the ceiling to let in the afternoon light. A magnificent gun collection was mounted at the far end of the room. The study furniture was done in various shades of hunter green and beige. A carpet, depicting an English hunting scene, covered the floor.

Sara was surprised at what a ruggedly handsome man Lord Derek was as he turned from the window to greet her. He was tall, lean, with shady blond hair and crystal sky blue eyes that turned blue-green when he smiled. He was muscular in his forearms, back and shoulders. He had a dimple in his chin when he smiled and she felt like a young school girl again in his presence. He was wearing an off-white ruffled shirt open almost to his waist showing a mass of dark brown curls and buckskin pants and knee high boots of dark brown leather. He was by far the most handsome man she had ever seen.

Her gaze finally ended up on Derek again. It was then she realized with a start that he resembled Captain Berne. She hadn't realized it immediately, for he was dressed in finer clothes. There were subtle differences, of course, but to anyone not real familiar with both men, she could see how one young man could easily pass for the other.

Sara curtseyed before him and Derek raised her gloved hand to his lips as she rose. Their eyes met and in that instant both of them knew they had found the one true love they had been searching for.

Shelby knew that he could not tell her that he was not Derek. He knew a woman as fine as this would be honor bound to obey the agreement entered into by their families. He needed time for her to get to know him as a person before he told her the truth. Perhaps she would marry him then.

Sara likewise knew that she wanted this man desperately as she had never wanted any other man. She was also wise enough to realize that he would probably not be interested in her if he didn't think she was Alexis. She decided that she needed time to win him over before she told him the truth. After all, if Alexis were still alive, she was out in the middle of the ocean with Captain Berne, who would most certainly find out sooner or later who she was. There was no reason for her to tell Derek and ruin her own chance for happiness.

"You are more beautiful than I dreamed," Shelby told Sara.

"And you are more handsome than I dared hope," replied Sara.

The two gilded lovers walked out to the terrace and descended the marble staircase to the gardens below. They spent the better part of the day walking the gardens and talking about themselves. It was obvious to the household servants that the two had fallen deeply in love.

That evening after an early dinner, Shelby walked with Sara down to the landing and around the lawn to where a gazebo had been erected. The air was filled with the smell of the early spring rosebuds. Shelby took Sara into his arms and bending his head slightly to meet her parted lips, kissed her deeply.

Sara had never kissed a man before and was totally unprepared for the helplessness that Shelby had aroused in her. She almost swooned as his lips met hers. His hands slowly slid up her arms and he ran his hands caressingly over her breasts. Sara was powerless to stop him. An emptiness filled her for want of him.

Shelby took off his jacket and laid it on the floor as he gently guided her to it. As much as Sara wanted him, she felt that she must confide in him and tell him who she really was. After all he was a Lord and had a great responsibility to his family and country. Although she loved him, she couldn't trick him into this type of situation. It was better that she told him who she was first, and then if he still wanted her she would give herself to him.

Breathlessly, her voice barely a whisper heard above the night sounds, Sara pushed her hands against Shelby's bare chest. He ignored her protests and kept up his pursuit by stroking her neck while raining hot kissed over her face and the tops of her breasts. He had skillfully undone the top of her dress. She caught his hand and removed it from beneath her dress.

Shelby was not to be deterred. He knew she protested because she was still a virgin. He had pinned her beneath him and, blazed a trail of smoldering kisses upon her throat and lips. Sara rallied all of the strength she possessed and pushed Shelby back.

"Please, please stop, we must talk first," she wept.

Shelby couldn't figure out why she cried out when he knew she felt as he did. "What is wrong, my darling? I know you love me as much as I love you. I can see it in your eyes. I know you were not brought up as simple maiden and I

139

know you feel a sense of pride and responsibility to wait to make love to me until we are wed, but my love, our wedding date is already past due. I have grown weak needing you and thinking of you."

"Please Derek, we must talk before this goes any further." Sara sat up and straightened her dress.

Shelby rose and held out his hand to her to help her rise. Arm and arm they walked down to the wharf and sat at the edge of the embankment. As they nestled against the bark of an old willow tree, Sara said, "Lord Derek, please believe me when I tell you that I fell in love with you the moment I saw you. In all honesty, I never expected this to happen. After all, I am not a young girl anymore." Sara lowered her eyes as they had filled to the brim with tears as she spoke. "Sir, I beg your forgiveness, but I must confess I have deceived you. I am not Lady Alexandra Leighton. I'm sorry."

As the tears started to stream down her soft powered cheeks, Sara started to rise to flee back to her room to pack her things and return to Charlestown and eventually to England. She had not only failed Lord Spencer and Lady Alexis, but herself.

Shelby was momentarily caught off guard. Off all the things she could have said to him, this was not what he expected. He swiftly caught her wrist before she could escape him and pulled her slowly back down to the shimmering blue green lawn. He cradled her in his arms. Her body racked with the tears that she hadn't been able to shed during her ordeal at sea. Shelby held her close until he felt she was spent of emotion. He gently raised her head to force her to look into his eyes. He bent his head and kissed her lightly on the lips.

"Who are you really, my love? Do you have a name?"

"I am Alexis' Aunt Sara. Lord Spencer is my half-brother through our father's second marriage after Lord Spencer's mother died. Lord Spencer was already married and on his own when I was born. After Lord Spencer and Lord Thomas executed the betrothal agreement, I was asked to come and help prepare Alexis for her marriage. I guess I really haven't done a very good job of it."

"What happened to the real Alexis, or is she trying to get out of this marriage?"

"Get out of the marriage? Why would you suggest such a thing?" Sara implored.

"Sara, my love, I have a confession to make." He turned from her and wrapped his arms around his legs as he stared out over the river. "I am not Lord Derek." He turned slowly as he spoke so that he could judge her reaction. As he did, he smiled impishly at her. He felt like he did when he was young lad and had been caught with his hand in the cookie jar.

142

Sara was surprised, but she just as quickly saw the humor in the situation and she stated to laugh. Shelby couldn't resist her infectious laughter and joined her. It was then that the irony of the situation hit them.

"Sara, this means that we don't have to feel guilty for feeling the way we do. We are both free to do as our hearts tell us. That is if you are free?"

"Yes, I am free," Sara replied. She leaned over and took his head between her hands and brushed a kiss against his brow. Caught off guard, but not to be out maneuvered, Shelby pushed Sara slowly back onto the grass and kissed her soundly.

"What name are you known by my love?" Sara whispered in his ear as she nibbled gently on its lob.

Shelby leaned back on one elbow and as his finger traced the outline of her face, he said, "I was christened

Shelburne Torrance Craven, the Earl of Clarkson. It's not much of an estate. The estate belonged to my mother's younger sister. When my Aunt passed away, she left it to me since I had no inheritance of my own. It is not elaborate by Lord Derek's standards, but it is lovely and it is mine."

"If you're not Lady Alexis, then where is Alexis?" Shelby inquired with a raised brow.

"I'm not sure. You see we were attacked by pirates and left drifting with a broken topmast. We were later rescued by the Charming Madam."

"You said you were rescued by the Charming Madam?" Shelby inquired as he sat up suddenly alarmed.

"Why, yes," replied Sara. "Why?"

"The Charming Madam is one of Derek's ships. Why didn't you tell me you met the real Derek? Boy, what a fool you must have thought I was parading as Derek."

"No you are mistaken Shelby, no one by that name was on either ship. The Captain was a Captain Berne. Oh, he was a handsome man. In fact, you look very much like him. I really didn't get a chance to see him up close or talk to him as Alexis cut him up pretty bad with her sword. If only she hadn't insisted upon facing the pirates head on. When I first met you, for a minute I thought you were him, Captain Berne. There are subtle differences of course, but you still look a lot like him."

"Cut him up, my god Sara. What happened? Is Derek alright?" Shelby sat upright and had suddenly become alarmed. His face clearly showed his concern. He grabbed Sara by the shoulders as he spoke.

"Shelby, please. Derek wasn't on the ship. I don't know what you're babbling about. Alexis drew her sword on one of the mates. After she severed most of his arm, another man, the Captain, started to duel with her. She drew blood several times, finally hitting him, um… you know, hit him real good…to where he dropped to his knees in pain, but before he hit the deck of the ship, he swung at Alexis and hit her hard enough to cause her to pass out. Oh, all that blood. It was awful. I though Alexis was going to get us all killed."

"Sara, was the Captain alive when you last saw him?"

"Yes, I believe he was. You see, Rocky was the person that gave all the orders for a while. He said the Captain was in bed recuperating from his wounds. Alexis was dressed like a boy and when Rocky went below to treat her wounds, he found out he was a she. He advised Caren and I not to say anything to the rest of the crew as the Captain would be really upset being laid up by a girl."

"Does the Captain know that Alexis is Alexis?' inquired Shelby.

"No, I don't believe he does. Why?"

All of a sudden Shelby started to laugh. He rolled over several times on the ground and had to hold his sides to keep from totaling losing control. Sara looked on helplessly trying to determine what was so funny about Alexis and Captain Berne sword fighting with each other?

Sara slowly rose and walked over to where Shelby was sitting. She sat down beside him and put her arms around him. He was still trying to regain control over his senses. He finally turned to Sara and taking her hands in his said, "Sara, Derek is Captain Berne. It's the name he goes by when he is on the open seas. He left Wynchester when he received his father's message regarding the betrothal agreement. He left me here to meet Alexis and try and get her married off or at least bedded before he got back so that he could cry foul play on her part and not marry her. In his attempt to escape her, he not only rescues her but lets her best him in a duel. Oh make no mistake woman; my cousin will truly be embarrassed by his actions. Although it serves him right for deserting the poor girl in the first place. He should have been here waiting for her."

Now it was Sara's turn to get excited. "You mean Captain Berne is Lord Derek? The Lord Derek Alexis is supposed to marry?"

"Yes, my love."

"But, they don't know each other by any other names than Captain Berne and Willy."

"Willy?" asked Shelby.

"Yes, Willy. We decided to keep her identity a secret in case we were attacked by pirates again. We didn't want anyone kidnapping Alexis and holding her for ransom. The last time I saw Alexis she was still parading around as a boy. I know the Captain didn't know who she was or he would have ravished her for she is very beautiful."

Before Sara could utter another word, Shelby pushed her back onto the carpet of mossy grass now damp with the night's dew and kissed her soundly.

Willy and the Sea Captain

Chapter 9

As nightfall settled over the ship, Willy said good night to Captain Berne and Rocky. She had no intention of sleeping on the gently swaying vessel when land was so close. She felt the need and comfort of solid ground. She also felt it was necessary to put some space between herself and the Captain. She was apprehensive at the fervor of the Captain's passion. She knew the fanaticism she was experiencing was caused by her own inexperience when it came to relating to a man. While the Captain was handsome, gentle at times, and very persuasive, she knew it would not be possible for them to ever marry and have a life together. Her family would never accept a sea captain over a member of England's nobility.

She walked quickly to her cabin, opened the door, slipped in, and slid the bolt in place behind her to delay the Captain from finding out that she left the ship. She slipped out of her dress and donned a pair of britches. She slipped a silk

Sandra Lee Chapp

shirt over her head, and pushed one of the small trunks in her cabin over to the port hole.

Quietly, she climbed up on top of the trunk and cautiously slid out through the port hole. As she hit the water, she held her breath momentarily under water in case someone on deck heard her. When she was sure no alarm had been raised, she started breast stroking swiftly towards the shore. With the help of the current she was able to reach the sandy beach within a few minutes.

She walked down to the waterfall where she had bathed earlier to retrieve her comb and bath soaps. Untying her hair, she brushed the tangles out and let it hang loose so that the warm breeze would blow it dry. She stripped off all of her clothes and hung them over a pine tree branch to dry. She gathered leaves and needles into a mound for a bed so that her silken skin would be protected from the ground. She dared not build a fire for fear of the Captain seeing it from the ship. Hot coals from the cooking fire she made earlier were still radiating enough heat to ward off the night chill. She laid down on the mattress she had made and immediately fell into a deep sleep.

Captain Berne's body still ached from the warmth of Willy's body and his nostrils were filled with her scent. He decided that he must be with her tonight. After all, he had been at sea for several months. He was mesmerized by her beauty. It was hard to believe she had drawn a sword on him and had actually been successful in wounding him. He rubbed the area surrounding his manhood, as the pain returned each time he recalled what she had done to him. He decided that she needed to be taught a lesson. She must have had some pretty bad experiences at the hands of the pirates who attacked the ship before he found her. He would reawaken her passion and remind her of how beautiful and rewarding passion could be.

He instructed Rocky to take the first watch and he would relieve him at midnight. He turned on his heel and headed for his cabin. As he walked along the hall he paused outside of Willy's door. He knocked gently on her cabin door. He could feel his heart pounding in his chest. He was at a loss to explain why she affected him like this. When there was no answer, he took ahold of the door knob and turned it. Placing pressure on the door he soon realized that the door had been bolted from within.

Feeling rejected, he turned and headed for his own cabin. This wisp of a maiden totally mystified him. She was the first woman he had ever met that he didn't quite know what to expect from. He felt certain she would be anxiously awaiting his advances this evening. He crossed over to the port hole in his cabin and gazed out across the sea. For a moment he thought he saw her swimming in the sea, but knowing she was safely locked in her cabin, he shook his head to clear it of her image and turned toward his bed.

Willy and the Sea Captain

Captain Berne spent a restless night until it was time to relieve Rocky. He kept seeing Willy in his dreams. She was standing before him with open arms and each time he reached for her she would evaporate into thin air. What kind of a spell had she cast on him? How could he love her when he was already committed to someone else? He needed to talk to her about returning to the Colonies with him and becoming his mistress. He knew he could offer her a much better life than the one she previously had been living.

As the opaque mist drifted upwards to let in the morning sun, the Captain stretched to relieve his cramped muscles. He felt sweaty from the previous day's activities and decided to slip ashore before waking Rocky.

He bundled up a change of clothes and carried it to the boat he used the night before to row ashore. The sea was calm and it took him only a short time to reach the beach. He pulled the boat ashore and walked down the trampled path leading to the waterfall he remembered seeing yesterday where he found Willy and helped her carry the evening meal to the beach. He rounded the path leading down to the water and stopped dead in his tracks. Before him was a vision of sheer purity and loveliness. Willy was poised on a rock preparing to dive into the water. He watch transfixed as she cleared the rock. Not wanting to frighten her, but rather catch her unaware and join her, he slipped into the woods and circled the pond to a point behind the waterfall. He slipped out of his clothes. Desire filled every nerve and played havoc with his senses. As she turned her back to him, he dived into the water. He dove in after her and caught her around the waist in his hands as she was preparing to surface.

Willy, thinking she was alone and that some sea creature had attached itself to her, reached for the gripping force that had entrapped her. As she struggled to free herself, Captain Berne remembered just in time to trap her legs to keep her from kicking him and inflicting serious harm on him. He turned her around and kissed her before she could make another sound.

Still fighting his advances, she felt her body betray her as all resistance flowed from her when his lips met hers. She reached up and entwined her hands into his hair and returned is kiss with the same intensity that he was giving to her.

He lifted her out of the water and carried her to the mossy bank. As he laid her gently on the ground, his hands caressed her torso. He leaned over her and licked the pooled droplets of gleaming water from her face. Willy moaned and arched her back. This only inflamed him more and encouraged him to continue his plunder of her.

Willy knew she had to get herself under control or risk losing everything. Breathlessly, she begged for him to stop, grabbing great handfuls of his hair and pulling his head up. Captain Berne saw the fear in her eyes and moved atop her and gently kissed her. "Willy, you have no reason to fear me. I am not like those other men who ravished you. Let me love you."

"No, no, you mustn't. I have never lain with a man before. I am betrothed to be married. Please get off of me and let us dress and return to the ship before you do something you'll regret." She balled up her fists and began beating him on his chest.

"No, my precious mermaid, I cannot stop now. I know you are hesitant and scared because of the damage done to you by those pirates, but I promise you that it will be alright. Relax and let me love you as you are a woman who was made for love making. Your body and emotions are giving you away. You know deep in your heart that you want me as much as I want you."

As he bent to kiss her soundly, Willy screamed and bit his tongue. He gazed into her tear filled eyes and held her close while she cried herself out. "Do not be afraid, I will make everything better for you."

"I shall never forgive you for what you have done to me Captain and I shall kill you at the first opportunity I get. You will never escape my wrath for you are trying to ruin my reputation. I cannot let your assault go unrevenged." With that she shut her eyes and braced herself for what may come. Her body went rigid beneath him and she turned her face from his penetrating gaze.

Captain Berne was shocked by her behavior and her apparent refusal to enjoy his advances. He tried unsuccessfully to coax her out of her apathy by whispering endearments to her and by caressing her breasts. He kissed her ear lobes. He knew by how she responded that she had closed him out and shut down.

When she awoke, she found herself cradled in his arms. He was affectionately looking down at her and smiling. For all she had been through, she felt at peace with herself and smiled back at him. He looked straight into her crystal blue eyes and knew she would accept what fate would befall on her. He lifted her chin slightly as he kissed her tenderly on the lips. "I am truly sorry for what happened. I cannot take back what I have done, but I would like to call a truce for the remainder of the voyage. You are the first woman I have known who is capable of making me feel rotten for wanting to love you. I want there to be tranquility and harmony between us. You are so beautiful and so young, and yet for all your inexperience, I have never met a woman like you."

Willy blushed profusely. She raised her eyes to his and asked, "Why me?"

The Captain laughed as he caressed the side of her neck trailing his fingers lightly over her shoulders. "I think my little mermaid that you were made for me. I think you have a very passionate nature if only you would let yourself relax and enjoy our time together."

"What makes you think I shall enjoy you and be able to satisfy your needs, my lord?" asked Willy.

"Because my needs are also your needs, my love. You will not be able to keep yourself from my bed for long, as you are a woman made for loving," replied Captain Berne.

Willy reached out and touched his brow. She loved him with all her being. She wished she could have met him under difference circumstances. "Do you have a first name my pirate captain?"

"My given name is Derek, Derek Berne." He wished he could tell her more, but he knew the truth would only hurt her and he was not ready for her to scorn him yet. If she knew he was a member of English royalty in his own right she would know life together with him was futile. His eyes clouded over with the thought that right now, his future wife waited for him at his plantation.

Willy caught the faraway look in his eyes. She wrapped her arms around him and pulled his head down to her so she could kiss him on the check. He was a little startled by her aggressiveness, but quickly recovered.

She caught him off guard and rolled off the blanket they were on. She dressed quickly and prepared to go back to the ship. Captain Berne knew he had said and did the wrong thing. Although he did not want to argue with her, he felt he should see the record straight so that she wouldn't worry unnecessarily.

"Willy, I know you are concerned about how you will face your family when we reach civilization. Do not continue to torment yourself. Although I cannot offer you marriage, I will be happy to provide for you. You shall have servants, beautiful dresses and fine furnishings. I will see that a proper amount of money is set aside for your personal use."

"You cannot offer me marriage. You think you are better than I and deserve a more important bride, perhaps one of noble birth? How dare you speak to me this way." She caught him in the left eye as she swung at him with all her might. He had not anticipated this outburst and was unable to back away before her fist connected with his eye. As she swung at him again, he backed off her to keep her from hitting his other eye. She quickly picked up a handful of dirt from the ground and flung it in his face, blinding him and choking him on it.

As he rolled over trying to get out of her reach, she grabbed a stick and began hitting him on the buttocks. He tried to grab for her or the stick, but could not maintain his balance because of her quickness and the fact that his vision was still blurred by the dirt she had thrown at him. Before he could regain his balance, she rushed at him and knocked him over backwards into the pool.

By the time he surfaced and was able to clear his eyes, she was gone from the clearing. He decided to finish his bath as long as he was already wet, and dove under the water to rinse himself off. He could feel his left eye starting to swell shut. He rubbed his buttocks where she had left large welts from smacking him. Derek decided he had best dress and return to the ship for medical attention before his eye got any worse. He would send Rocky back to find her and bring her back to the ship later in the day after she had a chance to cool down.

As he walked from the water, he realized she had taken his clothes. He searched around the surrounding area thinking she might have discarded them nearby. It became embarrassingly apparent that she had taken them with her. Suddenly he realized that she may try and take the boat. He raced from the clearing to the beach only to find out that it was to late. The small row boat was gone. She must have headed back to the ship to lock herself back in her cabin before he got there.

It was then he realized that her door was locked when he left the ship that morning. Since he lowered the first boat, she must have swam ashore earlier. He was going to have a talk with her when he got back to the ship. He couldn't have her flaunting his authority in his face. When he gave an order, it was supposed to be carried out. Taking a few deep breaths, he waded out from the island until he could no longer touch bottom and began the swim back to the ship.

After Willy pushed Derek into the pond, she quickly grabbed all of his clothing and headed for the boat she felt certain the Captain had brought with him and left docked on the shore. She knew that if she was ever going to get home, she needed to find another ship to sail on. She decided hastily, that she would row out beyond his reach until nightfall. She would then return to the island to gather provisions. By early morning, she would be well on her way to try and find a passing ship to take her to England or the Colonies.

Rocky did not see the little craft leave the island, so he had no way of knowing in which direction she rowed. He was equally surprised to see the Captain climb aboard in the buff sporting a black eye that had already swollen shut and a half dozen large welts across his buttocks. Rocky was the first to speak up, "Why Captain, did you run into a shark or by chance was it a little red headed mermaid, hee, hee."

"Hush Rocky. Fetch me something for my eye and these welts. I'll be in my cabin dressing. You had better be quick about it. As soon as you finish dressing my wounds, I want Willy gagged and bound, and brought to me. I will see that she is punished properly."

"But Captain, Willy ain't here."

Willy and the Sea Captain

The Captain turned and walked off the deck and failed to catch any of Rocky's words.

Oh we are in for it now thought Rocky. I knew a woman on board was bad luck. I am going to be in a heap of trouble when the Captain finds out Willy ain't here. I best lower another boat and go ashore and try and find her.

Chapter 10

Alexis rowed with all her might, not even taking time to finish dressing as she left the little island that she had once thought of as a paradise. She steered the little boat off to the west and around to the far side to the island. She had decided not to wait until nightfall to get provisions. She felt her only chance to survive would be to get as far away as possible from the island before Derek started searching for her. She knew he eventually would come after her and drag her back to the ship if only to satisfy his lust.

Derek had hurt her pride when he asked her to be his mistress. He made it quite clear that he did not consider her good enough to be a sea captain's wife. If only he knew she was the daughter of an English Lord and betrothed to a Lord who would one day become a Duke. Lord Craven, besides being a British noblemen, had property on both sides of the ocean and owned several shipping vessels. Who did Captain Derek Berne think he was dealing with, some maid.

In a highly agitated state, Alexis bathed quickly on the beach and finished dressing. She decided to revert to a young lad again until she was sure she would not fall into the hands of pirates again. She took Derek's shirts with her to use as carrying packs for the fruits and vegetables she intended to gather and take on the boat with her. She wrapped the remainder of Derek's clothes with the rest of the garments he brought with him and stored them in the bottom of the boat. She was glad he had remembered to bring his sword, knife and gun with him. It would afford her some protection should she be attacked.

She set off to gather potatoes, yams, carrots and assorted fruits and wild berries that she saw yesterday while walking around the island. She doubled back to the waterfall to retrieve the pitchers that she had filled and left there the day before. She gathered eggs that had been laid by the wild hens that populated the island. She gathered several branches that she thought she could shape into crude weapons, and picked up several stones to fashion tools out of.

When she loaded all of her make shift provisions into the boat, she cast off, not turning back to take one last look at the island. She rowed vigorously all day until dusk when exhausted and sore she ate some of the fruit and a raw potato. She unwrapped Captain Berne's clothes and fashioned them into a pillow of sorts and laid down in the bottom of the boat to rest. She covered herself and the boat with the tarp Captain Berne's clothes had been wrapped in.

Alexis dreamed of Captain Berne and the strange feelings he evoked in her. She dreamed of her father and her brothers and the hopes and dreams they had for her when she first left England for the Colonies. She wondered how Sara was doing and if she was worried about her. She tried to imagine how her betrothed took the news of her capture by a renegade pirate ship and their disappearance in the storm.

She awoke once during the night and realized she had been dreaming of Captain Berne. For all she had been through, she had to admit to herself that she missed his touch and the feelings he evoked in her. Perhaps if she had stayed with him longer, he would have learned to truly love her. It was early morning before she finally fell into a deep sleep.

She awoke with the sun shining brightly overhead. She wondered how far she had drifted and if she was anywhere near the Chestergate. She ate a light meal and spent most of the day just letting the craft drift while she tried to fashion tools and weapons out of the wood and stones she had with her. Before long she had constructed a lance and some small arrows and a bow. She used the lances from Derek's boots as string for the bow.

She tried her hand at fishing and was rewarded by catching a pink salmon. She cleaned the fish carefully and sliced the salmon into strips. She didn't realize how hungry she was until she began nibbling on the ripe bits. Alexis found herself dreaming and thinking of Derek often. She wished he was here with her now and was holding her in his arms. She laughed as she remembered what Aunt Sara had told her about men. Wait until she got home and told Sara how wrong she was.

Her heart began to palpitate in her chest when she realized she could not tell anyone about the Captain and what he had done to her. What would her family think? In addition, she had instigated further dalliance by her own actions.

At last she fell into a deep and restful sleep which lasted until early morning the next day. Just before dawn, she was awakened by the sound of waves splashing against the side of the boat. She became instantly alarmed as the boat was listing heavily to one side. She pulled the tarp back and was shocked to see that she had beached sometime during the night on land. She had no idea where she was, but she was certain this was not the same island she and Derek had been on. She jumped out of the boat and pulled it farther onto the shore until she was sure it would not drift back out to sea. She set out on foot to explore her new surroundings.

The island was surprisingly green and profuse with wild flowers of every color and scent. Colorful birds chirped in the trees and swans glided lazily over the crystal blue water. Butterflies flirted with her as she walked along the sandy beach.

Mid-morning she came upon a town. It was built on the side of a hill. Its buildings were made of white alabaster with shingled roofs. The town appeared to be well developed and even had a wharf with several large ships in the bay. She sauntered over to the market area and asked one of the marketers where she might find the Governor. She was surprised that he spoke fluent English, and responded by telling her that the Governor's home could be found at the top of the hill.

As she started her walk up the twisting road, she was able to overhear enough of the local chatter and gossip to understand that she had landed in the Bahamas, which were controlled by the British Crown. Her spirits soared with the good news. She would be able to send word to her father of her rescue and ask for his help in returning to England.

When she finally reached the home of the British Governor, she walked up the front drive, knocked on the door and waited for someone to respond. The door was opened by an elderly gentleman. "Good morning, sir. I am here to see the Governor."

He inspected her from head to toe, and responded by asking her, "Do you have an appointment, sir?"

Willy and the Sea Captain

"Why no, I don't. In fact, I just arrived." She pulled her hat off to let her hair fall down her back so that he could see that the young lad standing before him was a she. "Tell him Lady Alexandra Leighton is here to see him."

"Lady Alexandra, you sure don't look like a lady. I feel it is my duty to warn you miss, if you're not who you say you are, the Governor will have you arrested and thrown in jail."

"I am fully aware of the probable penalties facing someone who impersonates a member of the personage. I assure you I am who I say I am. Now please hurry."

"Yes, madam, if you will please have a seat while I announce you."

Clicking his heels, the door man turned and left through a set of double doors at the end of the entry hall.

Less than two minutes later, a middle aged woman came rushing into the hall. "O my God, I don't believe it. Alexandra, what in the world are you doing here? Does your father know where you are at? He was beside himself with worry when he received word that your ship was missing at sea. What happened to you, you look dreadful my dear."

At the sight of the wife of one of her father's oldest and dearest friends, Alexis broke down in tears. Lady Stephanie took Alexis in her arms and led her into the front parlor and over to one of the settees. Sheltering her protectively in her arms, Lady Stephanie sat with Alexis until the flow of tears stopped. Giving her a handkerchief, Lady Stephanie helped Alexis dry her eyes.

"Now my little lamb, tell me what happened, and don't you leave anything out. I can't help you unless I know all of the facts."

"Oh Lady Stephanie, it was awful. It was my father and Lord Thomas' idea that I marry Lord Thomas' son. I didn't want to and prayed that I would be saved from such a terrible fate. I guess God was punishing me for having such thoughts."

Lady Stephanie's brow wrinkled when Alexis mentioned that she didn't want to marry Lord Thomas' son Derek. She had known Derek much longer than Alexis and knew that he was an outrageously handsome man. "Have you ever met Lord Thomas' son whom you seem to dislike immensely?"

Alexis replied, "No, in fact, that is why I wanted to postpone the marriage. I wanted to give the young Lord Craven a chance to court me. Let us get use to the idea of being together." Alexis broke down in tears again. How could she tell this dear friend of hers the ordeal she had been through and the fact that now Lord Craven would never be able to marry her?

"Now, now my dear, it can't be all that bad. It's best you get it all out now. Why you'd frighten your dear father if he saw you like this. I think perhaps something to eat and a nice hot bath would help relax you, and then we can talk more if you like. Give me a few minutes to get your room ready."

Lady Stephanie left the room to go and prepare a room for Alexis. She also instructed one of the maids that was about Alexis' size to go into town and buy some garments for Alexis and to bring back the dressmaker back with her. By the looks of Alexis' clothes, it appeared she had lost everything in the ship wreck.

Lady Stephanie walked back to the parlor and took Alexis by the hand and led her upstairs to a room at the far end of the hall. It overlooked the gardens in the back of the house and was shady in the afternoon providing for a cool atmosphere. The maid had already opened the French doors and a gentle breeze was coming in. The room was done in pale yellow silk with a mint green rug. A large canopied bed was positioned opposite the French doors and was covered in a saffron eyelet fabric. The maids had placed a large brass tub near the open doors and were already busily filling it with hot water.

"Alexis, do you mind if we scent your bath with lilacs?"

"No, in fact, that sounds deliciously perfect." Alexis slipped off her clothes and stepped into the tub. She didn't realize, until she hit the water, how tired and drained this ordeal had made her. One of the maids shampooed her hair for her while she lathered up her arms and breasts. As she was finishing her bath, Lady Stephanie returned carrying several packages. A maid carried in a tray of assorted sandwiches and lemonade and set it on a table near the fireplace for Alexis.

Lady Stephanie insisted Alexis wrap in a towel and sit down to eat while she unpacked the boxes. Alexis was overwhelmed by the lady's generosity.

"I'll see that my father repays you for your kindness Lady Stephanie."

"Oh, my dear, you know how I do love to spoil you young ones. I won't hear of you repaying us. You've done that already by coming to us for help in your hour of need. I've already spoken to my dear husband, Lester, and he has written your father. He is also checking to see when the next ship to England will be in port. I know I haven't asked you, but I felt that because of your trying experiences, you would probably rather return home first before going to the Colonies to meet your betrothed."

"Yes, I would like to go home," replied Alexis. She waited for the maids to clear the room before she continued, "Lady Stephanie, I really need a lady friend to talk to, but I must

Willy and the Sea Captain

ask you not to repeat what I tell you, not even to your husband. I think you will understand after you hear my story."

"Why yes child. You can tell me everything and then you and I can decide what we will tell the menfolk."

Alexis got up and went over to sit on the edge of the bed with Lady Stephanie. "The trip started off well. Aunt Sara, Caren and I had been a sea for about three weeks when one foggy morning we were shot at by pirates. The Captain sent us all below. Aunt Sara was afraid the pirates would rape us unless we pretended we had the pox. She remembered that I was allergic to strawberries and so she and Caren rubbed me down with a strawberry poultice and soaked by hair in kerosene. Just as they finished, pirates boarded the ship and broke into the cabins, raping and killing the passengers and crew on board."

"When they broke into our cabin, Sara hollered pox, pox, pox. The pirates immediately become alarmed and abandoned the ship. They fired a cannon ball into the mast before leaving. The ship caught fire and we thought we were going to have to abandon ship, but the rain came and put the fire out. Caren, Sara and I disposed of the bodies that were still on board the following morning."

Tears trickled down Alexis' face as she continued her tale. "We drifted for several weeks after that until one morning we heard someone board the ship. I quickly dressed as a young lad and went up on deck with my sword in hand. When I reached the deck, I was greeted by a pirate who I quickly dispatched. Then another pirate, that I later learned was the Captain of the Charming Madam, started dueling with me. I got several good spars in and wounded him severely in the groin area. Before he passed out, he sliced by breast with his sword. I passed out for a while and found myself being treated by the ship doctor, Rocky, when I came to."

"Shortly after my recovery, The Captain made me climb the rigging. I lost my balance and fell into the sea.

181

Willy and the Sea Captain

The Captain jumped in after me and carried me back to his cabin. I had just fully recovered when a storm came up and caused us to be separated from the other ship."

"The following morning we came upon a small island. We rowed ashore and had dinner there that night. The Captain made us all go back to the ship before dark, but I crawled out a port hole in my cabin and swam back to the island. I just had to sleep on land again. You have no idea what it is like trying to sleep on a ship all of the time. Well, the Captain realized I was missing and came after me." Alexis stammered and again broke down in tears.

Lady Stephanie rocked Alexis gently in her arms while she waited for her to cry herself out. Her mind was contemplating the alternatives available to them. What would dear Alexis tell her father? Oh, what a mess this situation was, but thank God the lass was still alive.

When Alexis finished crying her heart out, Lady Stephanie gave her a drink laced with a sleeping draught to help her sleep for a while. "My dear, you are obviously exhausted. Drink this down and rest awhile. I will come back to see you when you wake up, and we will discuss your future. I also think it would be a good idea for the island doctor to come and check you over. Sleep now, my little one."

Alexis laid back on the pillows and closed her eyes. Lady Stephanie covered her with a comforter and kissed her on the forehead. She turned and quietly closed the door to Alexis' room.

Alexis slept the rest of that day and night and awoke refreshed the following morning. She was served breakfast in bed and just as she was finishing the dressmaker arrived to take her measurements.

Lady Stephanie sat on the couch near the fireplace chatting away and looking through the swatches of

Willy and the Sea Captain

material the dressmaker brought with her. "Oh, Alexis you must have a dress in this magnificent indigo. I could loan you my sapphires to wear with it."

"But Lady Stephanie," Alexis laughed, caught up in her mood, "Where would I possibly wear such a dress here on the island?"

"Why Alexis I must have forgotten to mention that the Annual Governor's Ball will be held next month and since you'll still be here with us, I do hope you will come and give the young maidens on this island some competition."

"Oh, yes Lady Stephanie, I would love to come. It has been so long since I have been to a ball." Looking at the material Lady Stephanie had chosen, Alexis said, "What a perfect color and style you have chosen for me. It seems like forever since I've worn a dress such as this."

After picking out a dozen or more patterns and fabrics, Alexis dressed in a riding outfit that Lady Stephanie had purchased from the shop in town. Lady Stephanie than escorted Alexis out to the stables to pick out a horse to ride. Alexis found a golden Arabian stallion. Lady Stephanie chuckled when she saw Alexis' selection. "My dear, you are only the second person who has ever attempted to ride that horse. I hope you know what you are doing."

"I think I can handle him. He is such a beauty." Alexis was stroking the nose of the horse and feeding him sugar cubes from her jacket pocket. "What's his name Lady Stephanie?"

"Heros, after the legendary Greek hero. You are only the second person since he was brought here that he has allowed to get anywhere near him."

"I shall take very good care of him, and I think he will enjoy the exercise. Don't worry about us, Lady

185

Stephanie. We'll probably be gone for several hours." With that remark, Alexis mounted the horse and was off.

She rode up into the hills behind the estate and soon came upon a valley of rolling grass. She let the horse have its head as they raced as one over the plains. They covered several miles when she finally pulled back on the bit to slow the horse down. She spotted a small creek ahead and led the horse to it to drink. She dismounted from the horse and tied the reins to the pummel of the saddle, letting the horse roam free to feed on grass and clover. She sat by the creek and found herself picking stones from the bank and tossing them into the water.

Her life seemed to be more orderly again as she realized she was safe now and would soon be on her way back to her father. Outside of deciding what she would tell him about her not being able to wed Derek any longer, she felt her life was finally getting back to normal. Perhaps her father would let her buy a small farm near his estate or even give her a few acres away from the main house where she could live when she wasn't traveling.

Picking a blade of grass near the stream, she leaned back in the grass and chewed on the blade while pondering about what she would tell her father. He would be devastated if she told him she had been assaulted by a pirate. Perhaps she would explain that she had fallen in love on the ship coming over with a wealthy Colonial landowner who was later killed in the pirate attack. Yes… the more she thought about it the more she liked that idea. She would be a grieving widow. In this fashion she could return to England and her family and save face. It would also allow Lord Derek to wed a girl of his own choice.

Alexis spent the rest of the afternoon exploring the hills and caverns around the Governor's estate. As the sun was beginning to set, she made her way back to the stables.

Willy and the Sea Captain

The month before the Governor's Ball went by quickly. Alexis spent most of her days out riding. She had written letters to her father and Lord Derek explaining her situation. Although she had not had a return message from her father, Lady Stephanie had been able to secure passage for her on an English ship that would be docking soon.

The morning of the ball, Alexis was busy having the final fitting on her new gown. Lady Stephanie had been in and out of her room several times that morning smiling and talking to herself. She told Alexis that she had a surprise for her. Alexis smiled and asked her what it was. Lady Stephanie just shook her head and explained that she would find out that evening.

Alexis spent most of the day in her room resting and preparing for the ball. Lady Stephanie came to her room just as the first guests were about to arrive and asked Alexis to join her in the receiving line.

Sandra Lee Chapp

"Oh Lady Stephanie, you don't need to include me in your receiving line. I'll be happy to circulate around the room while you and the Governor are receiving guests."

"Nonsense, my dear. I want you there beside me to meet everyone who's been invited. I won't have it any other way. Now come my dear, the guests are starting to arrive and I have someone who just arrived this morning that I especially want you to meet. In fact, he will be the Captain of the ship the Governor has booked you passage on. His ship is in port to pick up trade goods, but you should be able to get under way within two to three weeks. Anyway, you look absolutely stunning in that gown. I knew you would look good in that color as soon as the dressmaker showed me the swatch of material."

Alexis did indeed look stunning in the midnight blue silk taffeta gown. The neckline and skirt were a glow with beaded sapphires. Alexis wore a slim necklace of sapphires and diamonds with matching bobs on her ears.

189

Alexis walked beside Lady Stephanie as they descended the grand staircase. At the bottom of the stairs she could see the Governor talking with someone. She could not see the other person as he was partially hidden by a wall hanging. As Lady Stephanie approached, the Governor looked up and stepped forward to take her hand. "My dear, you look lovely tonight, and Lady Alexandra, how beautiful you are."

The Governor turned to the gentleman he had been talking to. "Lord Derek, I believe you know my wife, but have you met Lady Alexandra yet?"

Lord Derek turned with a smile on his face to greet the ladies. As he saw Lady Alexandra, he was momentarily startled. He quickly recovered and smiled as he kissed the ladies hands.

Alexis had been looking at the front door where some guests were coming in and did not catch the Governor's introduction. As she felt a familiar touch and kiss upon her hand, she turned to find Captain Berne before her holding her hand. She gasped and fainted.

Derek caught her before she fell to the floor and quickly picked her up and carried her into the parlor. He assured Lady Stephanie and the Governor that she was going to be all right. He told them that he would stay with her and for them to go ahead and receive their guests. He would bring Lady Alexandra around and stay with her until she felt fully recovered. Laughingly, he said, "You know I always seem to affect women this way. I guess it's my dazzling good looks." He winked at Lady Stephanie and added, "I guess she wasn't prepared to meet her fiancé."

Lady Stephanie blushed. "No Lord Derek, I thought I would surprise you both. But somehow you didn't seem quite as shocked as she was. Now you go easy on her, she has had a very rough time of it these past few months. If she doesn't tell you herself tomorrow of her adventures, I will."

Willy and the Sea Captain

With that she grabbed her husband's arm and walked from the room closing the door behind her.

Derek walked over to where Willy was lying and knelt before her. He kissed her lightly on the lips and brushed a few strands of her hair from her face. He laid his head upon her bosom and murmured to her, "Oh Willy, why did you leave me. Why didn't you tell me who you really were? I can't believe you are not only the girl of my dreams, but also my betrothed. Who would have ever guessed that you were the daughter of my father's best friend? Can you ever forgive me my little golden mermaid?"

Alexis wasn't sure what happened to her or where she was at. As she made her way back from the enveloping darkness, she thought she could hear Captain Berne whispering to her. As her eyes fluttered open, she saw him.

As her heart began pounding in her chest she frantically whispered, "Captain…Captain Berne. What are you doing here? How did you find me?"

"Ah I see your regaining your color again. Do you frequently have these fainting spells my dear?" he chuckled. He bent over her and kissed her softly on the lips.

She felt her body shake with desire as he kissed her. Her lips melted with him. She unconsciously brought her arms up to encircle his neck while she caressed his hair with her hands.

"Were you as surprised to see me as I was to see you, and did I hear the Governor call you Lady Alexandra?" he smiled.

"How did you get in here? How did you get the Governor to help you? Get off me you big oaf." Alexis pounded on his chest.

Willy and the Sea Captain

"Is that the way to treat your future husband my dear?" He grinned as he looked down at her. "Do you know how worried I have been about you? You really scared us disappearing in the boat like that. Do you realize that real pirates might have found you again before I did?" He ran his finger tip gently down the side of her check to her lips. As he bent to kiss her again, she pushed him back.

"My future husband you say! What kind of a fool do you think I am?" She quickly swung her legs around and sat up before he started to kiss her again.

Derek grabbed her hand as she started to rise from the settee pulling her back towards him. "Willy, please. We need to talk," he pleaded.

As she turned to look at him, she said, "Why...I've heard it all. You made it very clear to me that I was only good enough to be your mistress. Now that you know I have a title and dowry you think this is your big chance to win a rich wife. Well, don't sit here spewing terms of endearment to me, you jack ass. How did you get in here, after all you are just a common sea captain?" She turned her nose up at him and turned away from him.

As she started walking to the parlor door Derek didn't know quite how to respond to her. He was shocked by her tone and was hurt by her words. He hadn't realized how much she hated him for what he had done to her. He had been so happy to see her safe that he had forgotten his earlier pledge.

He rose to his feet and in several long strides caught up with her before she reached the door. "Willy, I mean Alexis, please...we must talk. Please...I promise not to touch you, if you'll just come back and talk to me. You have a lot of explaining to do as I do. Please..." he looked at her imploringly. His dark eyes piercing through her.

She lowered her eyes from his gaze and whispered a soft yes to his plea. She walked over to the French doors that opened onto the patio and opened them and walked out into the warm night air. The stars were already brightly shinning in the sky. She turned back towards Derek as she reached the railing. Folding her arms in front of her and leaning back against the railing she said, "You wanted to talk, so talk."

"Willy," he said.

"My name, as you well know, is Lady Alexandra. I prefer that you stop calling me Willy and start using my proper name."

"Yes, Lady Alexandra." He offered her a slight bow as he said her given name. "Lady Alexandra, let me introduce myself, I am Lord Derek Craven, your betrothed. It is a pleasure to meet you my dear." Derek's eyes sparkled as he said the words and stared at her waiting to see her reaction.

Sandra Lee Chapp

Although she had her doubts, she decided to challenge his statements, "You are not Lord Derek... You are Captain Berne."

"I'm both my love. I don't want anyone I meet on the high seas to know of my noble birth, so when I am at sea, I go by Captain Berne. I am Lord Craven. Your beautiful when your angry, Alexandra. I do love you, you know." Derek turned and walked to the other side of the patio.

"I was angry when you first ran away from me, but then I became very worried about you. Rocky and I searched for you for over a week. We stayed by the island thinking you would return. When you didn't, a part of me died. I never thought I would see you again. I am so sorry for the wrong I have done you and I do love you Alexandra with all my heart. I want us to be married immediately. I want to take you back home with me as my wife."

197

Willy and the Sea Captain

He turned now to face her and as he started to reach out for her she turned and walked away from him.

Softly she spoke, "Derek, I told you on the island that I would get even with you. When you asked me to be your mistress, I thought I would die of embarrassment," she whispered. She turned to face him and continued, "And now I find out that you were cheating on me when you weren't aware of who I was...and now you have the audacity to ask me to honor our parents' agreement and marry you."

She clenched her fists and continued with gathering fury, "How dare you be so bold. You cheating, conniving skunk. Oh! Captain Berne, Derek, Lord Craven, whoever you really are, hear me and hear me well. Stay away from me. Don't you come anywhere near me or I'll tell them all who you really are and what you are really like." She turned on her heal and walked through the patio door to the parlor, closing the door behind her.

Derek was shocked by her outburst. He thought she would understand once he had a chance to explain. Apparently, she didn't believe him or his behavior had affected her more than he thought. He truly missed her and loved her. It was better now that she was his betrothed because he could have a wife and lover that he truly cared for. No matter what she thinks, the marriage agreement still stands and he intended to force her to agree to it if she didn't come around. He planned on being in port for several weeks. He would try and woo her during that time and make her accept him for who he was. He admitted their relationship had gotten off on the wrong foot, but he would make it up to her.

Derek returned to the ball and spotted Alexis in the receiving line. She glanced up at him, but quickly turned away when she realized he was looking at her.

Willy and the Sea Captain

Alexis's heart was pounding. Who knows what?
Did Lady Stephanie know he was Captain Berne? Alexis did not
think so or she wouldn't have invited him.

After all the guests had come and the receiving
line was breaking up, Lady Stephanie took Alexis aside and
explained that she sent for Lord Derek because she had known
him and his family since he was a baby and she sees him
frequently when his ship is in port. She assured Alexis that he
was a man of great understanding and integrity and that Alexis
should confide in him about what happened. Lady Stephanie felt
knowing Derek as she did that he would accept Alexis as his
bride to be.

Alexis lowered her eyes so that Lady Stephanie
couldn't see what she was feeling and thinking. If only Lady
Stephanie realized that Lord Derek and Captain Berne were one
and the same. Derek said he loved her and wanted to marry her.
Was he sincere or obligated by duty? After all she had been

through she wanted to make sure she married for love and not convenience or the betrothal agreement.

As soon as she and Lady Stephanie entered the ballroom arm and arm, Derek approached her and asked her to dance. Lady Stephanie encouraged her to go ahead and spend time with her fiancé. As soon as she stepped into her arms, her whole body started tingling. No matter how much she tried to deny it, there was a strong chemistry between them.

Derek whispered in her ear that he would talk to her about what happened tomorrow afternoon after the ball. He wanted her to relax and enjoy the evening. He needed to make her understand who he was. He wanted to find out how she ended up here on the island.

Alexis agreed to go riding with him the following day. After dancing a set with Derek, Alexis danced with several other of the young men and local landowners invited to the ball. Derek managed to catch up with her right before the couples entered the dining hall for dinner.

When they entered the dining hall they realized they were seated at the head table with the Governor and Lady Stephanie. After everyone was seated, the Governor rose to propose a toast.

"On behalf of my dear wife and myself, we welcome you to our home. We have two very special guests with us tonight, may I introduce Lord Derek Leighton and his fiancée Lady Alexis Craven. Lady Alexis has been our guest for the past month and we have enjoyed her visit immensely. Please join me in congratulating them on their forth coming nuptials."

A cheer and round of applause went up through the dining hall. Lord Derek stood and addressed the crowded room. "Thank you for your warm welcome and joyous wishes. I am a very lucky man indeed." Alexis forced herself to smile and appear to be the happy bride to be, however, conversation at the table was forced and she could not wait for dinner to be over so that she could beg off and return to her room.

Derek was being the perfect gentleman and tried to see to her every need during dinner. Derek asked her to please join him for the first dance after dinner. She tried to plead fatigue, but he begged her for just one dance before she retired. "Everyone will be expecting to see the happy couple together." She finally agreed, not because Derek asked, but because she did not want to embarrass Lady Stephanie.

As they glided across the dance floor, the crowd moved back to watch them dance. Derek was quite surprised that she was such an accomplished dancer. He asked her teasingly, "When did you have time to learn to dance between sword practice and studying defense tactics?"

She replied, "My father felt I should be well rounded on and off the dance floor." Derek replied, "Obviously he spent more time teaching you to fight. Why?"

Alex replied, "My mother died giving birth to me. I had older brothers and so it was easier for my father to let me learn and train with the boys. I'm glad he did because it came in handy on the voyage over here."

Derek replied, "Yes, I still have bouts of pain from where you attacked me."

As soon as Alex could gracefully slip away she did. She sought out Lady Stephanie and begged her forgiveness as she was retiring. Lady Stephanie said she understood and let her go. Shortly thereafter, Derek took his leave and returned to his ship. Before he left he asked Lady Stephanie if she could have her cook prepare a picnic basket for him and Alexis for lunch tomorrow as he intended to court her and get to know her better. Lady Stephanie was delighted and agreed to have a meal prepared. She kissed him on the check and bid him good night.

Alexis tossed and turned all night. All she could think about was Derek and how he was Captain Berne. She wanted him, but not because he was Lord Derek. Could she love Lord Derek as much as she had Captain Berne? Did Captain Berne treat all women as he did Willy? He had a lot of explaining to do. She finally fell asleep as the sun was rising.

Lady Stephanie knocked on her door at noon. It was long past time for Alexis to be up. Alexis dressed quickly in her gold suede riding outfit. She still had mixed feelings about Captain Berne/Lord Derek.

Derek arrived shortly after lunch. He looked magnificent in a royal blue riding outfit. Lady Stephanie was waiting in the parlor with him until Alexis joined them. As promised, Lady Stephanie had cook prepare a picnic lunch for them.

Lord Derek greeted Alexis with a bow and kissed her hand. He asked her if she would be more comfortable riding in an open carriage rather than on horseback. She declined. She opted to ride Heros. This was yet another surprise for Derek. Most women preferred riding in a carriage instead of on horseback. He was further surprised when he found out that Alexis rode astride instead of using a side saddle.

It was a beautiful day for the outing. The sun was shining and a cool tropical breeze was blowing. The couple headed down the coast to the beach. About a half hour into their ride they came across a corpse of trees with a grassy spot large enough to spread a blanket and partake of the lunch the cook had prepared. Up until they stopped for lunch, not much had been said between them. There seemed to be a comfortable silence between them. Each lost in their own thoughts.

As they settled down to eat, Derek started talking first. He assured Alexis that he would not try to touch her or bed her before their wedding. It was his greatest wish that she agree to marry him. He proposed that they return to England for the wedding so that both families could be present. Until now, she remained silent. She knew he spoke from the heart, she could see it in his eyes. As much as she wanted to go home and see her family, she wasn't ready for another long sea voyage after her last ordeal. She suggested they take time to get to know one another without all the drama of the last few months and see just how compatible they really were.

She asked him if Lady Stephanie knew he was also Captain Berne. He said yes she did, but she was sworn to secrecy. All of a sudden she let out a peal of laughter. No wonder Lady Stephanie had contacted Derek and asked him to come. She knew he and Captain Berne were one and the same. Derek asked, "What is so funny?"

She quickly explained that when she first arrived, she was so distraught that she told Lady Stephanie about Captain Berne. Now it was Derek's turn to turn red. He assured Alexis that Lady Stephanie never mentioned it when she summoned him that she knew what had happened on the open sea.

Willy and the Sea Captain

Derek took Alexis' hand and said, "We have such great chemistry together. I didn't think I was ready to settle down when my father's letter came telling me it was time to wed. Never in my wildest dreams did I think I would find someone to love and cherish as quickly as I did. I fell in love with you. Yes, my Willy, I do love you and have been tormented with worry about you these past few weeks. Forget the agreement our father's entered into. I want you to be my wife because I truly love you. Will you marry me?"

Alexis' eyes teared up as Derek spoke. She looked into his eyes and said, "Yes, my Lord, I will marry you. I fell in love with you on the ship. I ran away because I was afraid you didn't have the same feelings for me. I think of you and dream of you constantly. I still feel your touch when I close my eyes. I want you so much. I think we should be married here and then head for home."

Sandra Lee Chapp

Derek reached over and held her tight against him breathing in the fresh scent of her hair. He tilted her face up and kissed her soundly. "I agree we need to wed as soon as possible. Your father will be displeased if I get you with child before the ceremony," said Derek.

Willy and the Sea Captain

Chapter 11

Three weeks later Lady Alexis walked down the aisle at the local church on the arm of the Governor. Lady Stephanie agreed to be her matron of honor and Rocky served as best man. After a brief reception, the couple set sail for the Colonies and Derek's plantation Wynchester. He wanted to stop and see if Shelby wanted to sail back to England with them.

As they arrived in Charlestown, Alexis was excited to get her first glimpse of the Colonies. There was so much activity going on the pier and in the town. It was more civilized than she thought.

While Derek supervised the unloading of the ship, a messenger was sent to Shelby letting him know that they had docked, and to arrange for transportation to Wynchester. Alexis stayed on the ship while she waited for Derek to see to the cargo. Sometime later, a boat could be seen coming down the river. On it was someone who resembled Derek and a pregnant woman. As the barge drew closer, Alexis realized with a start that the woman was her Aunt Sara. As soon as she could she ran down the plank and ran to the dock where the boat was headed in and mooring. As the boat docked, she climbed aboard and threw her arms around her Aunt.

"What happened?" asked Alexis.

"Oh Alexis, please meet my dearest husband, Shelby. We met when I arrived in Charlestown and fell in love at first site. We married a short time later, and as you can see I am with child. I see you and Captain Berne finally made it. We were so worried about you."

Alexis smiled at her Aunt, "Congratulations my dear Aunt. You deserve so much happiness. As for me, my Captain Berne is also my husband Derek. Didn't Shelby tell you that Captain Berne and Lord Derek were one and the same? Let's go over and sit and talk, we have a lot to catch up on since you left the ship."

Chapter 12

Several months later two very pregnant young ladies arrived in London with their charming and dashing husbands. Alexis' father was there to meet them. He raced up the gangway as soon as the ship docked and embraced Alexis in a long hug and welcomed his new son-in-law into the family. He was surprised to see Shelby with Sara. At that moment, he thought of his wife and how much they both wanted to see this day happen. He knew she was smiling down on them from heaven.

Sandra Lee Chapp

Made in the USA
Lexington, KY
08 January 2013